Barbara Girion

A Tangle of Roots

CHARLES SCRIBNER'S SONS

New York

Copyright © 1976, 1979 Barbara Girion

Library of Congress Cataloging in Publication Data
Girion, Barbara, 1937–
A tangle of roots.
SUMMARY: Beth is stunned by her mother's
sudden death but soon realizes that she and her
father must adjust to their loss and begin a new
phase of life.
[1. Death—Fiction.   2. Fathers and daughters—
Fiction]   I. Title.
PZ7.G4398Tan   [Fic]   78-27243
ISBN 0-684-16074-9

1 3 5 7 9 11 13 15 17 19   V/C   20 18 16 14 12 10 8 6 4 2

Printed in the United States of America

For Heywood
who patiently waited for it all to untangle . . .
and
to the memory of his father, Samuel Girion,
who would have been so proud

One

My friend Joyce and I juggled our books from hip to hip as we waited for the bus. I was balancing my mother's old yearbook across my arm and we were trying to study it. Mother had taken Dad to the station and then she had to go to an early meeting, otherwise she would have driven us.

Union High School, Class of 1956. Joyce and I had just made Millburn's yearbook staff and we were digging up old books looking for ideas we could use.

The pages were filled with pictures of serious-looking boys in suits and ties and rows of girls with sweaters topped by little white Peter Pan collars. "Dickies," my mother said they were called. And peeping out from the dickies were the inevitable pearls, all alike, hanging midway between the collar and chest. My mother's were from the costume jewelry counter of a department store. Lots of her friends had real pearls, necklaces started when they were babies and added to each year.

My mother's eyes are dark; even on the printed page you

could catch their twinkle. Mine are too, but her nose is much straighter. I don't know how, but somewhere along the way the genes realigned themselves. I definitely have a bump in the center of my nose that doesn't seem to come from anyone in the immediate family.

We both have dark hair. Mine is long and straight. Mother's picture shows hair rolled to the shoulder in a page boy style with a big dip over one eye. The dip had a blond streak. Half the girls in the yearbook had those blond streaks. Mother said they were a big fad. Yet when I mentioned streaking my own hair, she hit the ceiling. I showed her the yearbook. "That's what I mean," she yelled. "Look how stupid we looked. Your hair is gorgeous." She gently smoothed my part. Mother could never sustain a yell. "Besides, you can't improve Mother Nature!"

Joyce read the poetic sayings that were written under each student's picture. "Get a load of this one." She pointed to a dark moody-looking boy whose caption proclaimed, "Dark eyes, curly hair, the answer to a maiden's prayer . . ."

"Were they for real?"

We read my mother's. "Janet Bernstein, class secretary. A graceful presence bespeaks a lovely soul . . ."

"That's not too bad. Your mother must have been pretty popular."

"If she was, she won't admit it. She says you got something nice written about you if you were a close friend of someone on the yearbook committee."

Joyce flipped the page. "I guess some things never change."

I had asked Grandma Bernstein, who lives in the first-floor

apartment of our two-family house, for her yearbook. I was treated to a two-hour tirade for my mistake—about how she had to leave school to help put her younger brothers and sisters through, which didn't seem fair to me. She also waved her fingers around a lot. "See these? See these twisted fingers?" Grandma's joints are so swollen she can't even get a ring on. She says it all began on the Lower East Side where she worked as a child in a buttonhole factory, on a machine that chewed up your fingers if you didn't move fast enough. Aunt Nina says it's arthritis. Aunt Nina is my mother's younger sister. She's twenty-eight and a New York model. She doesn't really live with Grandma but comes home occasionally to recover from a love affair or a runny nose.

Mother has a great shape. I wonder if she was considered stacked by her classmates. It's hard to tell from the yearbook pictures. The photographer concentrated on recording noble profiles rather than nubile bodies. Mother told me that all the girls wore padded bras. And if your bra wasn't padded enough you had to stick cotton in the tips to fill it out. She said the object was to have your breasts pulled up so high that the straps cut into your shoulders and the tips came to sharp points.

Now Joyce and I try for a natural shape. That is, ever since we've had breasts. Actually Joyce's came in first, but so did her molars. We've been best friends since we were little kids and she's always been ahead of me. Joyce has to wear a bra; she's just too bouncy without. I wear the softest one I can find. I just can't walk down the hall and have my nipples sticking up right through my polo shirt. Most of the girls don't care. They like it, in fact, say it's part of women's lib. I don't know. I sort of like a boy to meet my eyes first instead of my chest, but then I love poetry too. I try to keep step with my friends and save one step to walk my own way.

There was a loud blast behind us. We both jumped.

"Kenny Perna," yelled Joyce, "when are you going to turn down that horn?" Kenny. Ken Perna! I had been secretly waiting for him to come along. What can I say about him? He's a senior, I'm a junior, but he'll be leaving in January for early admission to the University of Penn.

We've been going together almost a year, not counting the two summer months when he worked in Maine as a counselor and I had to stay home and waitress at a swim club. Just looking at Kenny makes breathing difficult. He fits that corny saying in Mother's yearbook perfectly. You'd think I'd be one-hundred-percent sure of him, but it's hard to figure where his head is at concerning me. His life is all planned: premed, then medical school, then residency in orthopedic surgery. Like he has a map of the future with red pins stuck in it to show the steps along the way. I wonder sometimes if I'm one of those red pins or if I'll get pulled out of the map when he graduates.

He yelled through the window. "OK, girls, your chariot awaits. Enter please." That was Kenny. He wouldn't tie himself down to promising me a ride, but just when I was resigned to taking the bus he'd come along.

I slid in next to him. Joyce hopped in the back. Kenny and I didn't exactly kiss. It was more like a nuzzling of necks. Just the same it was enough to send a weak feeling down my backbone through my legs. Gave me the trembles, the same way my muscles feel after a couple of hard sets of tennis.

I rested my hand on Kenny's thigh and he covered it with his. Long tapering fingers. Terrific on a basketball court and in a biology lab. Not to mention what they did to me when we were alone.

He squeezed my hand. "Tom's having everybody over after the game on Friday. What about you, Joyce?" He looked through the rearview mirror. "You going?"

"If there's nothing better to do."

"After we beat South Orange? Are you for real?"

"Ha, you wish," she answered.

Kenny loves to be with people. He's a party person. I wonder sometimes why he picked me. He can walk into a group and take over the whole conversation. Since I've been going with him I haven't missed one important thing in school. I've got to admit it was a kick to walk in someplace and have the girls give me the once-over. Some of them would give their right arms to be with him. Oh, I've got credentials of my own, but it's so much easier being swept along with Kenny.

We spoke on the phone every day and had our private times too. We'd stop for a burger someplace, then go to his house or mine. Mother and Dad liked me to bring Kenny home. After a few hellos they'd disappear and leave the living room to us. As Mother said, "I'd rather have you in the house than parked out on some dark street where any maniac can get you both. Besides," she stopped and dropped a light kiss on my forehead, "we trust you."

I shifted the books in my lap. Kenny Perna isn't Jewish. Mother never said anything about it. Grandma Bernstein did, loud and clear. Grandma's Orthodox Jewish and her first words upon meeting Kenny were, "Perna? Is he a *shaygets?*" Which is a word for non-Jew.

I guess Mother and Dad didn't say anything because they really didn't think it important enough to make a fuss over. Though occasionally I got a snide speech about not mixing peaches and plums and two books on the Holocaust were left conspicuously on my night table.

I turned around to Joyce. "Don't forget, Joyce, Miss Brock is giving us a review placement exam this morning—on the poets we covered last term." Reminding Joyce of her schoolwork is like trying to convince autumn leaves to fall up. Joyce is convinced of the inevitability of life, as she calls it. Whatever will be, will be. What she has absorbed in class she takes with her. Anything else she deems unnecessary to exert herself over. As she puts it, "They should be happy I sit and listen to their boring lectures. Further reading I shall not do." And she doesn't. How she maintains her honor roll standing, I'll never know.

One night, to test her, I called up about one in the morning to see if she were studying. All I got was an angry Mrs. Dowling who assured me that Joyce had been sleeping for hours.

Kenny dropped Joyce off before he pulled into the school parking lot. "I'll wait for you by the steps." Joyce was a dreamy friend. She knew just when to stand by and just when to take a walk. Never jealous. Of course, she has had half of our class in love with her since kindergarten, so she really wouldn't be jealous of one Kenny Perna.

Kenny zoomed into the lot. An angled spot underneath a huge red maple was waiting for us. I've been a sucker for New Jersey's autumn ever since I read about Jack Frost painting leaves. The sun filtered through the softly blowing branches above us and shadowed rose-colored patches on the wind-shield.

We were wrapped around each other before the ignition key was turned off. His lips were so smooth. I had a minute's worry about mine. Sometimes I chew my bottom lip and it gets all chapped and peely. I wanted to be as soft as he was. Kenny kept kissing. I assumed that my lips must feel nice. His hand rubbed my back and started to work its way around slowly.

"Kenny, what if somebody's around?"

"So?" He barely took his lips off mine to answer. "What do you think they'll see?" I was silenced by the combination of those soft lips and gentle fingers.

He let me go and we just looked at each other. I was trying hard not to pant, although I was sure my heart must be quivering through my polo shirt.

One more kiss and he opened the door. We walked quickly to the front steps holding hands. Even when we let go of each other I still felt the pressure of his fingers.

"I'll see you later, Ken."

Joyce was waiting. We walked into the building together but parted at our lockers. I would see her in Miss Brock's English class.

First period was a study hall. I needed it to get ready for Brock's review. But I kept drifting away from Edgar Allan Poe and Coleridge's *Ancient Mariner*. I found myself writing "Mrs. Kenneth Alan Perna. Dr. and Mrs. Kenneth Alan Perna. Beth Frankle and Ken Perna." I'm sixteen and a half. Kenny's eighteen. The age difference is perfect. Not that I'm interested in marriage or children—at least not for years.

I suddenly understood the graffiti artist's desire to immortalize a surface. I traced my hand over the engravings that were already on the desk.

"Susie and Mike—Nov. 1973."

"Linda 973-4116."

"B. W. and R. S."

I wished that I had a pen knife. I tried to write "Beth and Ken" with my ball-point but it just smudged. The pen wasn't sharp enough to dent the wood of the desk. Maybe it was vandalism, but at that very moment—no matter what was going to happen in ten years or even in fifteen minutes—I wanted to capture forever the feeling I got from writing "Beth and Ken."

Two

The intercom buzzer rang in English III. I had been sweating over "Annabel Lee." Good sweating. One of those essay questions that you could write a book about: Point out the biographical coincidences that are obvious in Edgar Allan Poe's "Annabel Lee."

Miss Brock answered the antiquated ringing. "Beth, Beth Frankle. You're wanted in the office."

I was annoyed. Edgar Allan and I had great vibrations. We had really been rolling along. I covered my paper with my English book, sent Joyce the two-fingered peace signal, and took off for the office.

Aunt Nina was standing by the attendance desk with Dr. Walters, the principal, and Miss Carstairs, the school nurse. Aunt Nina's face stopped me. She had a fever blister on her upper lip, one of those real ugly ones. Red, scabby, oozing slightly. Aunt Nina never appeared in public unless she was perfect. Her hair was pulled off her face and there were purple blotches on those famous cheekbones. Dr. Walters was talking softly to her.

I realized what must have happened. Grandma Bernstein. Aunt Nina must have been home recovering from her fever blister.

"Aunt Nina?" They turned to face me. Aunt Nina's eyes and nose were wet. She reached out a hand to me and sort of gurgled something in the back of her throat.

Grandma Bernstein had been in and out of hospitals as long as I could remember. Heart, high blood pressure, diabetes. My mother had to keep a catalog of Grandma's doctors. This time it must be serious, or no one would come to get me out of school.

"What's the matter, Aunt Nin?" I was conscious of Dr. Walters and Miss Carstairs. My God, I wished Aunt Nina would blow her nose—she really was a mess.

She couldn't answer me, and Dr. Walters cleared his throat. I can still see the words he said. He spoke, but the letters seemed to print themselves in front of my eyes and I read them as he was talking.

"Beth, I'm terribly sorry but there's been a tragedy at home. Your mother . . ." I remember he stopped there and I thought, he said the wrong word. He means "grandmother." "Beth, there's no easy way to tell you. Your mother's dead." Aunt Nina was shaking her head in affirmation. She was still making those gurgling sounds in the back of her throat.

"Are you all right, Beth?" That was Miss Carstairs.

Now Aunt Nina seemed to clear her throat. "Beth, it's true. Oh, darling. She was at a meeting—she put her hand to her head and fell down. The doctors think—cerebral hemorrhage. She died instantly. No pain. Your father is on his way home. I didn't go into the city today because of . . ." She broke off and wiped at her fever blister with the edge of a sleeve.

"No." I remember saying that. "No." Very clearly. I'm very logical. You wouldn't think so from the way I act around Kenny, but Physics and English are my two best subjects. People don't believe that, but I always apply the same logic to both. "No." Again. They must be talking about Grandma Bernstein. My mother is Janet Frankle. She's thirty-eight years old and you could put her down in the middle of the Black Plague and she would walk through untouched. "No." I said it again.

Everyone had gone crazy. I knew it wasn't a dream because my nails were cutting into the palms of my hands—and if I could feel that, I wasn't asleep. Maybe it was a movie. I would run it again in slow motion backwards. Walk back out the office door up the stairs to the second floor, Miss Brock's English class. There was the mark between my fingers from my ball-point pen. Who said ball-point pens don't leak? Mine did. My fingers were smudged. Backwards into that desk with Poe and Annabel Lee, his bride, back to where "I was a child and she was a child in this kingdom by the sea . . ."

Aunt Nina took my arm. "We'll be all right. I've got to get Beth home to her father."

Dr. Walters and Miss Carstairs walked us to the car. Wait, I wanted to cry. They weren't going to let me rerun the morning backward to where the intercom had rung.

Aunt Nina jerked the car. She was sniffling. Her hair had come loose and was falling in her eyes. How could she possibly see to get us home? "Aunt Nina, my mother is really dead?"

"Oh, baby." The gurgling started again in the back of her throat.

"Where's my father?"

"He should be home now."

My mother dead? How could that be? It wasn't even lunchtime.

"Aunt Nina, stop the car. I have to go back to school. I left my lunch in my locker."

"Are you crazy? Your mother's dead and you want to get your lunch out of your locker?"

She was starting to scream. I wondered in one of the compartments of my mind if she had been smoking something this morning.

"Aunt Nina, will I go back to school tomorrow?"

"Beth, the funeral will be tomorrow. You won't be back to school for at least a week."

"So, don't you see . . . it's tuna fish. The whole locker will stink all week. The tuna fish will spoil."

"God, give me strength. Beth . . . baby, we'll be home in a few minutes. Just hold on."

"But I've got to go back to my locker."

Why couldn't she understand? I had to get the tuna fish sandwich. My mother had made it for me that morning. My mother. That morning. My mother who's dead from a cerebral hemorrhage. Only people on doctor shows get cerebral hemorrhages. It's something they made up on TV.

The front door was open. My father was sitting on the couch. My father, who rode the Erie Lackawanna every day to get to work, had got on the train carrying his attaché case, got off at Hoboken, gone through the turnstile, switched to the New York train, got to his office, and turned around and come back through the turnstile, through Hoboken, on the Erie Lackawanna and back to Millburn, New Jersey, because his wife had dropped dead of a cerebral hemorrhage. He was still holding his attaché case.

I started to feel the trembling. It was inside me somewhere, cold, like a giant icicle growing from the pit of my stomach and spreading to my hands and feet. I was afraid to walk into the room. My mother. Where was my mother?

"Aunt Nin, what did they do with my mother?"

"Oh, honey, she's not here." Aunt Nina started gurgling again. "The funeral parlor took her body right from the meeting. She never even made it to a hospital."

My father looked up at me. Or he looked up at the doorway where I was standing. I don't think he saw me. The trembling was getting worse. I had to force myself to put one foot down and then the other.

Grandma Bernstein was standing in back of my father. She had a handkerchief in her mouth and she was swaying back and forth. She looked as if she was screaming, only no sound was leaving her mouth. Or maybe no sounds were entering my ears.

Grandma started to talk. "Oh, Beth. What a terrible thing for a girl to grow up without a mother. My Janet. My Janet. The sweetest, most wonderful . . ." Aunt Nina walked over to Grandma. "Ma, stop."

Grandma kept talking. Even with the handkerchief stuffed in her mouth, the words tumbled out. And again as I had in school, I saw them written in front of me instead of hearing them. "She was the best wife a man could want . . . you'll never find anyone like her, Steve."

"Ma—please stop it." Aunt Nina was pulling at Grandma's shoulders, but it was as if someone had wound up a spring and the words kept spinning out.

"Nina, what a sister you had—always she stuck up for you even when you were little . . ."

"Ma—for God's sakes!"

"And a daughter—pure gold—pure gold my Janet was . . ."

MOTHER! I ran into her bedroom. She had left early for the meeting. The bed wasn't made. Her nightgown was on the pillow. I picked it up and buried my head in it. It was still warm. It was, it was warm. My mother couldn't be dead. Her smell. It still smelled like my mother. Everyone has a smell. Joyce and I used to kid about it all the time. But it is true. Everyone has a smell and this was my mother's. I can't describe it; it wasn't the sweetness from her perfume. But my mother's nightgown held the smell of my childhood.

I trembled the time away until the funeral. Grandma Bernstein insisted that Mother have an Orthodox Jewish burial. I wanted to tell her it was too late to appease God, but she had to have everything just so. My father didn't care. Gram had Aunt Nina soap the mirrors. Something about not looking at yourself. And then hard little wooden stools were delivered to the house. We were supposed to sit on them during Shiva, the period of mourning. Hard, uncomfortable, to remind us in case we forgot.

The night before the funeral I felt a familiar cramping in my stomach, as if someone were scraping a rake along the lining of my body. My period was a week early. "Nerves," Aunt Nina said.

Rabbi Morton spoke to us before the service. He had delivered the sermon at my Bat Mitzvah three years before. Mother had worn a yellow knit. The jacket was removable and she took it off at my party. All the kids had thought she was so pretty, and usually young kids don't bother about parents.

I tried to concentrate on Rabbi Morton. He was very hairy. He had a beard and sideburns and a mustache and the backs of his hands had long black strands of hair. He was sort of young and I knew he had a Ph.D. in history from Harvard and some other degree in psychology from Columbia and everyone in our congregation thought he was brilliant.

He kept telling me I had to be brave for everyone. For my father, for my grandmother, and for my Aunt Nina. I had to be brave. I had to be brave. I wanted to ask him, Why? In fact, I wanted to shout at him: WHY DO I HAVE TO BE BRAVE? My father had fortified himself with Scotch. He looked a little seedy because he wasn't allowed to shave during the mourning period. Aunt Nina had some makeup on her fever blister, but it looked smeary; you could still see the crust through the pancake. Grandma kept crying and crying. "WHY? Why did my daughter die? Why didn't God take me? Why did he take my daughter?" Everything was so clear to me, even the trembling in my body. I wanted to tell her: Grandma, I agree. Why didn't he take you? You are old and a nuisance. My mother had to drive you to the doctor all the time and Aunt Nina is a nervous wreck because of you. Why didn't you die instead of my mother?

MOTHER! I couldn't remember what she looked like. I kept

thinking of the white collar and pearls in her yearbook picture.

Joyce had hardly looked at me when she came to the funeral home. Kenny tried to squeeze my hand but I pulled back. We had been making out, oblivious to the world, when my mother's brain had split apart. All of my friends acted embarrassed. What do you say to someone whose mother has just died? I'm sorry?

The rabbi talked on. Then suddenly he pinned black ribbons on us, took a razor, mumbled a prayer, and slashed the ribbons. My grandmother let out a scream. He explained in his sermon voice that in the old days people ripped their clothes, but now we would wear these black ribbons for thirty days to show the world that we were mourning.

He put one of his hairy hands on my shoulder. "Beth, if there is anything I can do, anytime you want to talk to me, just call my office." That was his psychology voice. Surely, he must have noticed that I had completely split apart with my trembling. But no, I looked down, there was my body, all in one piece.

He murmured something about God's mysterious ways. I wanted to ask him, What God? But I was afraid if he heard that question he would completely dissolve and nothing would be left but those curly black hairs circling forever in space.

Everyone told us that the service was beautiful, the coffin was beautiful, the cemetery was beautiful, the grave was beautiful, the sun was shining, the day was beautiful. I remember the big black Cadillac. With a chauffeur. No, he was really the driver from the funeral parlor. The car was so plush, you could get swallowed up in the seats. I used to think this was the way I would go to movie premieres, back in the days when

I was a little girl and had a mother. To be swallowed up in a big black limousine. And now I was riding in one that was taking me to where the earth was going to swallow up my mother. MOTHER! What did she look like? Grandma hadn't let anyone look in the coffin. She had said it wouldn't be dignified. What did my mother look like? I couldn't remember. She used to look something like Aunt Nina.

The burial was a movie of a movie. Somebody pushed a clump of dirt into my hand. The rabbi said a prayer. Everyone started to cry when my father recited Kaddish. And then someone—I think it was one of the funeral directors—pried open my fingers and made me drop the dirt in the grave. I didn't look down. It was just a hole in the ground. My mother wasn't there. I didn't know where she was, but she wasn't there. Maybe she was still in her nightgown. I had taken it and hidden it in the bottom of my closet. When I got home I would take it out and smell it and maybe I would remember what she looked like.

When we got home, we had to rinse our hands with water before we went inside. All the neighbors had prepared food.

"Eat. Eat, darling, you look pale." Someone stuck a plate with a bagel and lox and cream cheese in my hand. My mother would have left out the lox. She knew I hated it. MOTHER!

Mrs. Benson was fixing a plate for my father. She was divorced, lived around the corner. Dad was seated on his little stool. His jacket was off and he had loosened his tie. His yarmulke was pushed to the back of his head.

I walked into the kitchen. Bakery boxes were stacked on the counter. Cake and candy and food platters and fruit and cards and tributes. People wanted to donate to good causes. In honor of the death of Janet Frankle. They whispered—what did she die from? If it was cancer they could give to the Cancer Society; if it was heart trouble, to the Heart Fund. I didn't know if there was any fund for cerebral hemorrhage.

Everybody talked so slowly, distinctly, as if I'd gone deaf. They breathed a sigh of relief when they left. It wasn't their death. They had done their duty.

My mother's plants spilled greenery all over the kitchen. Hanging from pots, on the floor, the windowsill. She was so good with them. I never even bothered to learn their names.

The last time she and Dad went away for the weekend, I wouldn't even water them for her. She probably knew; they were dried out when she came home. But why should I water her plants, just so she and Daddy could go off by themselves?

If it wasn't for me, I think she would have lived in the city. But she always said the schools were lousy in New York. So she suffered in the suburbs for me and I wouldn't even water her stupid plants.

The icicle that had been growing inside me seemed to splinter. A sharp piece stuck in my chest and the back of my throat. It was hard to catch my breath. There were three plants on the windowsill. I put them in the sink. I was going to water them. Then I caught a look at myself in the kitchen window. My nose. Now I would have to have a nose job. Aunt Nina and Grandma always said, "Fix her nose, Janet. Get rid of the bump. Fix her nose." That's why they tell you to cover the mirrors. It's true, you're not supposed to think of your nose at a time like this. But my mother had always said, "No! No nose job! She doesn't need it!" I had a nose that only a mother could love and now I didn't have a mother to love it.

I ripped the plants out of the pots one by one. I started to strip the leaves off, but that was too slow. I yanked the tops and there were holes in the dirt and the plants lay naked, their fragile white-brown roots exposed. I think I would have pulled out every plant in that room. My dead mother's living plants so neatly growing in her kitchen.

My father walked into the room. He looked at the dirt and tangle of roots in the kitchen sink. He didn't say anything, just put his hand over my wrist and gently unclenched my fingers. I had a plant half in and half out.

He opened a drawer and handed me a spoon. He took a fork for himself, from right out of the drawer. A spoon and a fork that we ate with. He started pushing dirt back into one of the flower pots. He handed me one of the plants. The roots dangled helplessly. "Plant it." I just held it tightly. He reached out to the strand of hair that had fallen in my eyes and tucked it behind my ear. I put the plant in the hole and he patted down the earth around it. He handed me another and pointed to the empty hole. I did the same thing. We worked together silently. There would be time later on to think about matching the plants and untangling them. Right now it was enough to get those bare roots back into the ground and close in the spaces around them.

Three

Somehow we got through Shiva, the period of mourning. One week . . . one week of sitting on our hard stools. Grandma and Aunt Nina would come upstairs so we could all be together. At night the onslaught began: relatives and friends coming to pay their respects. For the first few minutes everybody would stand around and look solemn. Then Grandma Bernstein would cry. "I can't believe it. I still can't believe it." My father sat in a daze. As for me, I couldn't believe it either.

Four days after she died, I woke up and couldn't find any clean underwear in the drawer. The words "Hey, Mom" were out of my mouth before I realized that there was no such person anymore. Dad did the same thing. He walked out of his room looking for a clean shirt. We stared at each other.

I found her wallet and looked through it, searching for the Chinese laundry ticket. It was one of those fold-out wallets with secret compartments and room for pictures and credit cards and all sorts of things. In one of the small pockets on the side, I found a baby picture of myself—I think everyone has the same picture—leaning with two hands on a pillow and a blanket over my head. The photographer's idea of a baby playing peekaboo. There was also a picture of me in a ballet costume. I must have been about eight years old. My hair is pretty straight and Mother had curled and curled trying to get it right for the dancing school recital. There I was, Baby Beth and then Dancing Beth dressed up in a pink tutu, posing in what I think was supposed to be fifth position.

That night Joyce came over. We went to my room to get away from the crowd. Joyce and I hadn't talked alone since Mother died. Usually we both flop on the bed. I did, but Joyce sat on the hard chair near my desk. We had trouble getting started. Usually we never have enough time to talk. We could talk all day, walk each other home from school, and then get on the phone ten minutes after we separated.

Joyce tried to give me the latest gossip. "Hey, Beth, you know Millburn won last Friday."

"Won what?"

"The basketball game—you remember, with South Orange?"

For a moment I had the same feeling that had come over me in the kitchen when I ripped up the plants. On Friday, my mother had been dead two days and my best friend, Joyce, expected me to be interested in who won a basketball game?

Joyce tried again. "Remember, Beth, you always said you were going to do your room over. I could go with you and we could pick out some material. My mother said to tell you, she'd be glad to help, you know. I mean, since your mother . . ." Her voice stopped.

Do my room over. The funny thing was, Mother had been after me to do my room over. "Come on, Beth," she'd say, "we'll go to Bloomingdale's and you can look at material."

A couple of times we were supposed to go and then—I don't know—something would always come up and we wouldn't make it. Besides, deep down, I guess I never pushed it. My room is babyish but I've always loved it. I have one of those canopied beds, with a white ruffled top and matching dust ruffle and a pink-and-white gingham spread. Even now I feel like a princess sleeping in that bed. I remember when I first got it. I was eight, the same year I had my picture taken in the pink tutu. Daddy had just finished helping Mom put the ruffle on top. We all stood back and looked at it in admiration. I just adored it. I announced, "It's a bed for a princess."

And of course Dad said something like, "For our princess—you're our princess."

I couldn't wait to sleep in it. Mother had picked out pink sheets and pillow cases. Everything matched. With all the pink-and-white flowered wallpaper, I felt as if I was sleeping in a rose garden. They both tucked me in, kissed me, and then left. The door was open slightly.

I tossed and tossed. I couldn't sleep. Maybe it was the excitement of the new bed. No, it wasn't that. This beautiful bed with all the ruffles that made me feel like a princess wasn't comfortable. I suddenly realized something was rolling around underneath me. I got out of bed and turned on the light. Underneath the sheet was a tiny ball that had been moving with the pressure of my body. I heard a giggle from the doorway and Mother and Daddy burst into the room laughing.

"Something's wrong with this bed, Mommy," I said in all seriousness.

"You bet there is," said Dad. Then they showed me the small marble they had put underneath the sheet. Mother hugged me. "When you were three, your favorite story was 'The Princess and the Pea.' So, since you have a bed like a princess, we wanted to see if the rest of you acted like a princess." We all laughed, they took the marble out, and I remember snuggling under my new pink comforter and watching the breeze blow the edge of the ruffled canopy until I fell asleep.

Joyce was still talking and I realized that I was ignoring her.

"So, Beth, I don't know what to do. I like Doug, but Tom is so possessive and I don't want to be tied down to just one guy."

She was back to boys again. Last week that was very important to me too. Well, not boys, but Kenny in particular. I tried to follow Joyce's reasoning. It was either feast or famine as far as boys were concerned—though with Joyce it was usually feast, since she constantly had two or three chasing her. With me it was different.

Kenny and I had met at a basketball game. Well, not really. We had met before and I had developed an instant crush. I would absolutely devour him on the basketball court. There might as well have been no one else playing. I just watched Kenny Perna dash up one side and back down the other. I never even noticed whether or not he had the ball, I was too busy watching those shoulders and how the sweat of his body made the thin jersey basketball shirt stick to his chest. Number 21. And the dark hair curled tighter and tighter as he ran. It was only when the crowd started to scream that I would realize he had sunk a basket.

One night I managed to be on the court near the locker room entrance as the team ran off in victory. Somehow I got the nerve to stick my hand out as Number 21 ran by. "Congratulations, Kenny, great game."

He stopped for a minute, breathing heavily, absolutely dripping with exertion. He squeezed my hand back, then said, "Thanks. Hey, Beth, why don't you stick around and we'll go out for something after I'm showered."

"Why don't you stick around?" Why don't you stick around? Since that night I'd stuck like glue. During school, after school, weekends. Everything was so perfect, except for the fact that he wasn't Jewish. But I really think Mother and Dad would have gotten over that . . . eventually.

Joyce was on her feet. "Beth, I've got to run. Now you're sure you're going to school tomorrow?"

I nodded. The week was up. Daddy was going to work, Aunt Nina was going back to New York, I was going to school, and Grandma Bernstein was going to start "taking care of things" for us.

Joyce leaned over and pecked me on the cheek. She gave me an extra tight squeeze on the shoulder. "Beth, I'm so sorry." Her voice started to quaver. "I mean, like I don't know how to say it, but I really thought your mother was terrific. She was great. And you've been super. Why, if my mother were to . . ." She stopped, realizing where the conversation was headed.

Again I felt the rush of anger that started in my head and in my feet and met somewhere in the middle of my stomach. Sure, she was going to say if it were her mother who had died she wouldn't know what to do. Well, it wasn't her mother, and it wasn't Kenny's mother, and it wasn't even Aunt Nina's mother. It was my mother and I didn't know what I was going to do either.

Aunt Nina knocked at the door. People were leaving and they wanted to say good-bye to me. I walked out into the living room. Thank God this was the last night. The last night of people staring at me, sitting around drinking coffee, bringing us boxes of candy and cake that we would never eat, and telling us how terrible they felt.

I smiled and said good-bye and thanked them for coming. Mrs. Benson took my arm and pulled me into the kitchen. "Beth, dear"—she opened the refrigerator—"I made a casserole for you and your father. You can use it tomorrow night or just put it in the freezer and you can heat it up later in the week." She grabbed for my hand. I remembered that her husband had left her a couple of years ago. She used to come around and cry on Mother's shoulder. I'd come home from school and find Mrs. Benson sitting in the kitchen, eyes all red, sipping the cup of coffee that Mother had fixed for her.

I didn't want to be rude, but I pulled my hand away. I hate it when people—strange people—touch me. "And, Bethie, if there is anything, anything at all I can do for you, or your father, please call me. I'm right down the street."

I didn't like her calling me "Bethie." No one ever called me "Bethie," even when I was little. I know she was trying to be nice, but something about the way she was acting was annoying. She squeezed my hand and I almost told her that my father hated casseroles, but I realized that she would never know if we ate it or not. Besides, this was the last night, so we wouldn't be seeing her anymore.

The apartment was quiet, Grandma Bernstein was still on the couch rocking back and forth, her lips moving silently. I realized that she didn't have an apron on. I think this was the first week I ever remember her not wearing an apron. A family in mourning doesn't serve itself meals. The first few nights, though, after the company left, Aunt Nina and I were left with a stack of coffee cups to wash. Then Mrs. Benson had brought over some paper coffee cups and plastic spoons that we could use and throw away.

Aunt Nina was emptying ashtrays.

"Nina, you don't have to do that." That was my father.

"I don't mind, Steve, really. It keeps me busy."

That was pretty funny. When Aunt Nina emptied ashtrays you had to vacuum up ashes for two days afterwards because she had to be so careful of her nails. She did lots of magazine ads for Darling cosmetics, where the nail polish matches the lips and the model stands with her hands in a prayer position against her matching rouge-covered cheeks. I noticed that Aunt Nina had a bandage on one nail.

"What happened, Aunt Nina?" I pointed to her finger.

"Oh, it's a catch in one of my nails. I'm trying to save it."

Aunt Nina still looked very pale, but her fever blister had cleared up. And today she was wearing eye makeup, so her face was much more attractive.

"What color eye shadow do you have on, Aunt Nin?"

"Russet brown, Beth. When you have shadows under the eyes you don't wear a bright color like green or blue. Brown tones down the shadows."

Aunt Nina certainly knew everything about makeup and clothes and stuff like that. I got a real kick from opening a magazine and seeing her picture.

She and Mom always got along. Even when Aunt Nina's picture was staring out from a magazine and she had loads of gorgeous men after her, she still wasn't happy. Most of the time she'd come crying to Mom with her problems.

"Unstable." That's what Grandma Bernstein always said. "How come I got a daughter who's a runaway?"

Grandma really meant "runaround," but sometimes she twisted her words when she was excited. "And all those men. Always the phone ringing. 'Where's Nina, where's Nina?' I give up with her already." And she would wipe her hands on her apron swiftly as if she were wiping Aunt Nina away.

Mother was the calmer-downer. "Now, Ma," she would say. "You should be proud to have a daughter as beautiful as Nina. And where else would you get the money to spend two months in Miami Beach if you didn't have a rich and famous daughter?"

Once I asked Mother, "Aren't you ever jealous of Aunt Nina? I mean, no offense, and I'm glad you're my mother, but, gosh, New York and the magazines and everything?"

Mother had just laughed. "Look, Beth, I've got your father and you," she made a little face, "and Grandma, of course."

If Aunt Nina was our New York celebrity, Mother was our local lady celebrity. She was President of P.T.A. when I was in the lower grades and she was a substitute teacher. I never really thought about what she did all day. I know she was busy. But she was always there when I came home at lunchtime and, since I've been in senior high, after school.

I hadn't been able to sleep all week. I mentioned it to Aunt Nina.

"Listen, Beth, you're going back to school tomorrow. I'll give you half a Valium, it'll help you relax."

I took the ashtrays away from Aunt Nina. I'm not too good at housework either, but at least I can dump ashes without my hands shaking.

Dad interrupted. "Thanks, Nina, but I don't want Beth taking anything. She'll be fine."

That made me mad. He hadn't spoken to me alone since that night in the kitchen with the plants. Not that it was his fault. We hadn't had a chance to be alone with all these people coming and going.

"Steve, half a Valium isn't going to hurt her. It'll just take some tension away so she can get some sleep."

"She doesn't need it."

"Why don't we ask Beth? She's sixteen, old enough to decide if she can take half a tranquilizer."

"I said no, Nina." He was getting louder.

Grandma rocked back and forth on the couch. "Her mother, she needs her mother."

"Ma, stop it." Now Aunt Nina was getting louder.

"No tranquilizers, Nina. Beth is strong, she'll make it. We'll both make it."

"You always make such a big deal over medicine, Steve. What do you have against Valium?"

"Nothing. You want it, you take it. Leave Beth alone."

"Oh, fine. I suppose you want me to leave her strictly alone. Maybe you don't think I'm a good influence on her?"

"You said it, not me, Nina."

They were really at it now. Talking about me and around me and over and under me as if I wasn't standing right there in the room. I waited for someone to stop them, but Grandma Bernstein leaned back against the couch and closed her eyes.

Tuned out. MOTHER! I realized that she was always the one who had been on guard, quieting angry words before the situation got out of hand.

"If you didn't run around so much, you wouldn't need Valium either."

"Listen, Steve Frankle, what do you know about running around? I'd like to see you stand twelve hours under hot lights trying to look gorgeous while photographers and makeup men are busy analyzing all your defects."

"There're plenty of jobs still open in factories. Why don't you apply?"

I'd had enough. I left a half-full ashtray on the coffee table. Margaret, our twice-a-week cleaning lady, had been coming in every day since Mother died. She'd be in tomorrow. Nobody noticed as I left the room. I took my dress off and lay down. All my dolls and the pink flowers on the wallpaper stared at me. I closed my eyes. I rolled from side to side trying to get comfortable. But now I knew for sure that I was no princess and it wasn't a hard pea that was keeping me from sleep.

Four

It was awkward at first, being back in school. Kids didn't know what to say, so most of the time they tried to avoid me. The teachers were nice. Dr. Walters, the principal, called me to his office and asked if there was anything he could do.

Come to think of it, maybe people weren't avoiding me, maybe I was avoiding them. I just felt so tired all the time. Couldn't concentrate on anything.

The fourth day back, Miss Brock asked me to stay after English class. "As soon as you're ready, Beth, I'd like you to take your makeup test."

For a minute I didn't realize what she was talking about. She saw my confusion. "The English test you were working on the day you were called home."

I had forgotten all about it.

"I know, Beth, you've come through a terrible tragedy. I want you to take an extra week to get yourself together." She looked down at the open pad on her desk. "Shall we say, next Thursday at 3:15?"

I opened my mouth, closed it, and opened it again. "Yes, Miss Brock."

She was shuffling pencils on her desk. My arms were wrapped around my notebook and I was hugging it so tight that the sharp edges pinched my rib cage.

Miss Brock reached a hand out and patted my arm. "Beth, my deepest sympathies to you and your family." She sat down and began writing. Interview over.

I stared at her lowered head for a moment and then left the room. My sympathies to your family and you'll take your English test next Thursday! I guess that's what they mean when they say life goes on. Edgar Allan Poe and Annabelle Lee had just been sitting around waiting for me to get through burying my mother.

Kenny was waiting outside. "Drive you home, Beth?"

"Don't you have basketball practice, Ken?"

"I can skip. C'mon." He steered me to the door.

"But, Kenny, you'll get in trouble."

"Forget it, I'm taking you home."

The sun was still warm for late October. I always put on my winter things too early. It's because I get tired of my summer clothes. I could feel drops of sweat at the top of my turtleneck sweater.

I slid into the car. Kenny waited a minute before he started the ignition. I knew he was waiting for our ritual nuzzle kiss. I just couldn't. The sun was in my eyes and I pulled down the visor on my side. Still the glare caught my eyes. Most of the leaves were on the ground now. The tree branches stretched bare and brown to the sky. But here and there a leaf hung tenaciously, a beautiful golden orange, refusing to let go.

The sanitation department had started to sweep the leaves into great piles at the end of each curb. I remember walking home from elementary school. Joyce and I would jump in the biggest pile we could find. The leaves would crackle and scatter around us. If a street sweeper were around, he would yell and chase us away. We would run giggling down the street to find the next pile to jump into.

"If you sit any farther away, you'll be on the outside."

"Kenny, I'm sorry." I moved closer so that our knees were touching. I looked down at my sweater where the black ribbon was pinned. I moved my leg so my knee wasn't against his.

He stopped the car with a squeal of the tires. We were in front of my house.

"Kenny, I'd ask you in, but I'm not sure where my grandmother is. And I may have to help her."

"It's OK, Beth, I understand." He stared straight ahead, hands tight on the wheel. "Will you be able to go to the game this Friday?"

"Kenny, I'm still in mourning."

"I thought you finished that week of whatever you called it."

"The Shiva period. Yes, Kenny, but for a full month we're in mourning. I can't leave my father and my grandmother."

"OK, I'm sorry I asked. It's just that I miss you." He trailed his finger over my shoulder.

"I know. I miss you too, Ken."

"Listen, Beth, I just feel so bad for you, I wish I could do something."

I didn't answer. He tried again. "You just take it easy, do

whatever you have to for your family. We've got plenty of time to be together. And, Beth . . ."

I looked up. He turned his face away and looked out the window. "Your mother was a really nice lady. I mean she was always great about us—you know what I'm trying to say."

Just when I thought I couldn't possibly have one tear left in my body, the back of my eyes filled up. I guess he did understand. Kenny didn't like to have what he called emotional conversations. Last year when Millburn lost the county basketball championship—and with it his chance for an athletic scholarship—he came out of the locker room after the finals, hair slicked down from the shower, and said, "Let's get something to eat." He never mentioned the game or how he felt the whole night.

He revved the motor. "I think I can go back and still make practice."

I felt bad when he said he was going back and I guess that wasn't fair to him. But somehow I didn't want to think of him dribbling a ball up and down the court as if nothing had happened while I had to go inside the house and face my grandmother.

"Thanks for driving me, Ken."

"It's OK, Beth." He still waited, his hands frozen to the wheel. I knew he was waiting for our good-bye kiss. It was another special thing we had. I'd lean over and kiss him while my finger would spell out "I LOVE YOU!" in the palm of his hand. Kind of like braille or something. I got a shivery feeling, eyes closed, as I spelled out my feelings. He did too. I know because he used to tremble when I got to dotting the exclamation point.

I opened the car door, hugging my books close to me

again. I knew I'd have a black-and-blue mark on my chest from that sharp point on my notebook, but at least it gave me an excuse for not reaching out and touching him.

He pulled away as I shut the door. Oh, Kenny!

There were a couple of late-blooming geraniums in our window boxes. The leaves were kind of dried-out looking and I pinched them off with my fingers the way Mother used to. Some of the stalks still had fresh buds on them. One good frost and they would be gone. It was almost Halloween. We never had geraniums left at Halloween. Grandma used to get furious because Mother would get a big pumpkin and some dried Indian corn and decorate the front of our house.

"Halloween is a *goyisha* holiday, Janet Frankle. What kind of example are you setting for a Jewish child, letting her celebrate All Saints' Day?"

Mother would laugh—though, come to think of it, she would have that same tightening of the jawline that Kenny had when he was upset. And what a battle when I'd dress up for trick or treating. Grandma wouldn't even open her door for the kids in the neighborhood. They would clunk up the stairs to the second floor, and Mother always had bags of miniature chocolate bars, lollipops, some sugarless gum, and pennies for the UNICEF boxes.

I adored Halloween. Until I was ten, I was a gypsy or a princess or sometimes a medieval queen. Being the queen was tough. Mother and Aunt Nin would make me a cone-shaped hat from cardboard and they would wrap gauzy scarves around it. I loved to look over my shoulder and see the ends trailing down my back. But when I had to run to keep up with the other kids, the hat would never stay on. It was also a great target for the older boys who would push it over my face and say, "Oops, sorry, kid."

I guess the gypsy costume was my favorite. I had a big full skirt that Mother made from kitchen curtains. And Aunt Nina had a bright red scarf that we wrapped around my waist as a sash. I usually wore one of my blouses on top and Mother always insisted on a sweater. But the best part was the jewelry. Mother and Aunt Nin would empty their drawers. I had ropes and loops of colored beads and pearls and chains and one old rhinestone choker which I was positive contained real diamonds. And long dangling earrings which tickled my neck as I walked along—though the earrings never lasted too long. They were clip-on and would begin to pinch before I had been to six houses. When Aunt Nina was home she would put my makeup on. Lovely gooey green eye shadow. She couldn't get it dark enough. I'd keep saying, "More, more, Aunt Nina." Then rouge for the cheeks, and Mother would laugh and say, "She's supposed to be a gypsy, Nina, not a clown." But Aunt Nin couldn't get my cheeks red enough as far as I was concerned. Then mascara—which burned and caused my eyes to run. But it was worth the suffering.

I used to stop and show Grandma how I looked, even though she didn't approve of Jews celebrating Halloween. But the first year I was a gypsy she turned to Aunt Nina. "Give me your black eyebrow pencil, Nina."

Aunt Nina handed it over and she and Mother exchanged looks and raised eyebrows over Grandma's head.

"You two American girls, my daughters. You can tell you've never seen a real live gypsy. You left out the most important part." And Grandma took the eyebrow pencil and made a perfectly wonderful beauty mark high on the cheek-bone under my right eye. I loved it!

"Oh, it's great, Grandma. It's great." I turned the other cheek. "Make one on the other side. Oh, please make one on the other side." The three of them laughed together and Grandma rubbed some of my rouge off. "No, no, Beth. One beauty mark. A true gypsy only has one beauty mark."

Mother laughed out loud. "C'mon, Ma, what do you know about gypsies?"

"Never mind what I know. You think I'm some kind of schnook? I know plenty about gypsies and lots of other things too."

She turned back to me, "Well, if you're going to celebrate this Christian holiday, you'd better get along before it's too dark."

I'd go off waving and trying not to trip on my skirt. One year I begged for high heels, but they went the way of the medieval hat and the dangling earrings. After one block of pinched toes I took them off and went home to exchange them for my sneakers.

I would have gone on being a gypsy forever, but in the fifth grade all the girls decided to be tramps. So away went the beads and the makeup and the flounces, and into my father's closet I burrowed, looking for old pants, ties, and shirts.

With my dark skin and my straight hair tucked under an old golf hat and some soot smudges on my nose, I was the perfect tramp.

It was time to go inside. Grandma was in our apartment again. She was hardly ever there when Mother was alive. Then she used to say she had to be invited.

"Oh, listen, Ma, don't stand on ceremony. Come up whenever you want to," Mother would argue.

Grandma would shake her head firmly. "No, ma'am. Even in my daughter's house, I don't go unless I've got an invitation."

She was in my room. I threw my books on the desk. "Hi, Gram, what are you doing?"

"It's almost winter." She had my closet door open. "I think we'll go through your clothes and see what you need."

I walked over to the closet door and closed it. Boy, she had some nerve going through my things. "Mom—well, Mom and I had just done some shopping. And I don't like to buy everything at once. The styles change too much. We buy—that is, I buy as I go along."

She pointed to the door. "But all I see is jeans and jeans and more jeans."

"That's what all the kids wear, Grandma."

"Your Aunt Nina could take you for gorgeous clothes— wholesale too."

It was amazing. Usually Grandma was harping about Aunt Nina. Now Aunt Nina was the good guy who could take me for some clothes. One of my books slipped to the floor. Grandma stooped to pick it up. She looked at the title and wiped it on her apron.

"And that Margaret, some cleaning girl. I don't know how Janet let her get away with it. She left today after only six hours. Slam, bang, one, two, three—no house can be cleaned so quick."

"Margaret's all right, Gram. You'd better not follow her around. Mother used to say, 'She'll get bugged about something and quit. Then we won't have anybody.' "

"So you've got hands. I've got hands. We'll clean it ourselves. I was ten years old when I arrived in this country. Yes, miss, ten years old. Nineteen hundred and sixteen. And at ten I took care of all my brothers and sisters, cleaned and cooked while my mother went out to work. And we had boarders too."

I tried to close the bathroom door. I managed, but Grandma's voice still carried through. "And I worked all through the Depression. When your grandfather and I got married, we couldn't even live alone. We slept on a little couch in the living room with his family. And to my family we sent money."

I ran the water as loudly as I could. When Grandma started with her "in the beginning" story she could go on forever.

"Thirty I was before I had your mother. Thirty years old, before I could afford to have a baby. Even then you think it was easy? And now, now . . ." Her voice was getting quieter. I could tell the tears were about to start. "Lou dead seven years, and now my oldest daughter. I can't believe . . ."

The phone rang. I opened the door quickly and ran to it before Grandma could pick it up.

"Hi, Beth?"

"Yeah, it's me. That you, Joyce?"

"Uh huh. Listen, Beth, the nets are still up on the courts at Taylor Park."

"They are?" It had been such a warm autumn, I guess the Parks Commission had decided to let people play tennis as long as possible.

"Yeah. Why don't you throw on something and I'll meet you in ten minutes."

"I don't know."

"Your grandmother there?"

"Yeah!"

"Well, she doesn't have to know. Tell her you're coming over to my house for homework or something."

I hesitated. We were supposed to be in mourning. I couldn't remember if tennis was considered to be too entertaining or not. But I did need some fresh air for my health. That settled it. I knew that when it was a question of Jewish law or your health, the rabbis always allowed deviation for health purposes.

Grandma had left the Depression years. She was back describing the tenement on the East Side and her mother's boarders, one of whom stole my great-grandma's wedding brooch, which had been meant to be handed down through the generations.

"Grandma, I'm going out."

"Where are you going like that, in such a thin shirt? Why don't you put something warm on?"

"No, Grandma. It was too hot in the turtleneck. Are you eating with us tonight?"

"What do you mean, Am I eating with you tonight? You and your father are eating with *me*. Who else is going to cook? You? Your Aunt Nina with her gallivanting and shenanigans? Your big businessman father? Of course we're going to eat together."

I left her redusting the clean apartment and hurried to the park to meet Joyce.

We had a great tennis match. Not that I played that well—but I love the twangy thump when the ball hits the center of the racket and shoots back over the net. Joyce kept me running from side to side. I managed to hold my serve, though, and even catch her with a couple of little dropshots.

We worked up a sweat and I felt loose and relaxed for the first time in two weeks. We headed for home, giggling and talking.

Joyce started it. "Let's cut across the back lots like we used to, Beth."

"OK." It's funny what you do when you're little. We probably took twice as long to get home trying to figure out shortcuts. But it was fun racing across backyards and hoping people wouldn't catch us trespassing.

As we wove in and out the yards, I spied a huge pile of raked leaves in Mr. Ewing's backyard. I took off like a bolt.

"Run, run, as fast as you can, you can't catch me, I'm the gingerbread man." I threw the rhyme over my shoulder.

Joyce came right after me. She was running quickly. Just as she was about to tag me I made a gigantic leap, right into the pile of leaves. Joyce didn't hesitate. She dove in right after me.

We tumbled together in the dry leaves, rolling over and over. We sat up, giggling like crazy, and I could see the sweat on her brow and on the bridge of her nose. Her short streaky gold hair had curled from exertion and formed curly scallops across her forehead. I scooped up a pile of leaves and poured them over her.

She sputtered as some of the dusty crumbles got in her eyes and mouth. "You rat! I just washed my hair." She lunged forward and tackled me. I could smell the warm sweetness of her hair and her skin felt soft wherever it rubbed against my own. She began to tickle.

"C'mon, Joyce. Stop! Hey, no fair. You know I'm ticklish." It was no use. She straddled me, still tickling with one hand as I giggled helplessly. Then she took a big handful of leaves with her free hand and stuffed them down the back of my tennis shirt. I threw her off and was ready myself with a handful to stuff down her back.

"Hey, you girls there! Hey! You two! Cut that out!" We stopped and looked up. It was Mr. Ewing at the kitchen window. "I just raked those leaves. Took me all afternoon. Now look. Go on, get out of here. Go home where you belong."

We ran off, laughing and pelting each other with the leaves that still clung to us. My hair was too long. I could feel it as I ran. It would be a mess of brambles and tangles tonight.

We cut through another yard and then slowed down as we reached the sidewalk. We were still laughing at each other. Joyce began hopping on one foot. She jumped over the lines in the sidewalk and began a familiar chant.

"Step on a crack, break your mother's back . . ." As she said the word "mother," she stopped. She looked at me wide-eyed, her mouth open in a wide oval as if she could suck back the word before it reached my ears and hurt me.

I didn't want to feel sad anymore. At least not for the next few minutes. I reached for her hand and began hopping myself. We linked arms and skipped together. I deliberately landed on a line and finished the chant. "Step on a line, break your father's spine!"

Five

*Two weeks went by quickly. Dad left early in the morn-*ing and came back late. Aunt Nina called a few times, but she was busy on a job and didn't come back to New Jersey. Grandma Bernstein took over our apartment. A few times Dad called and said he wouldn't be home for supper. Then I had to eat alone with Grandma. I felt as if the music had stopped, leaving me suspended backwards under a limbo bar.

I went to school, did my homework, and talked with my friends. Kenny still drove me home when he didn't have basketball practice. We had a date for the first Saturday following the month of mourning.

I'd be busy reading or humming when that sinking feeling would hit my stomach. I was still shocked when I opened the door to our apartment and didn't find my mother. All her things still hung in the closets. Grandma kept saying we would have to go through them and give them away. I kept waiting for Daddy to take charge, to tell Grandma to go back downstairs to her own apartment. I thought that when the month was up we would somehow go back to normal, though I still couldn't imagine what normal was without Mother.

The Friday night that marked the last day of the mourning period Grandma made a big Shabbes dinner. Daddy came home on time and even Aunt Nina came in for the night. We were all going to attend services at the synagogue together.

Dad was washing up in the bathroom. "Hey, Beth, did you see my after-shave lotion?"

I walked in. He was freshly shaved. There was a tiny piece of tissue stuck to his chin. Blood was oozing where he had nicked himself. Dad's about five-feet, ten-inches, and he has a nice build. He and Mother played a lot of tennis and he jogged whenever he had a chance. I noticed that his stomach looked a little flabby.

"And, Beth, do you know where my styptic pencil is?" He pointed to his chin. "I can't seem to find anything in the medicine chest."

I made one of my frown faces, as Mother would call it. "Grandma's been in here all week rearranging everything, Dad. Let me see if I can find it."

Dad reached for a towel. "And who put these little towels here? Your mother knows I like the big towels."

There was a stillness as we waited for the word "mother" to dissolve.

"Here's your styptic pencil. I don't know where Grandma put the after-shave. Maybe underneath." I bent down to look through the shelves on the bottom of the vanity. Grandma had been through everything in the past two weeks. The toothbrushes were neatly in the holders, although we never kept them there. We each had our own colors and put them on separate shelves in the medicine cabinet. Grandma had dug out all the fancy hand towels that Dad hated and hung them around the bathroom.

"Here it is." I emerged triumphant with the bottle of Aramis. "Don't feel bad, Dad. She threw out my hair spray and changed my deodorant brand this week."

Dad slapped on the after-shave. The smell filled the room. He smoothed a piece of hair back from my face. "Beth, I know how hard this is on you." His voice broke. He reached up and pulled the paper from his chin. "OUCH!" The bleeding started again.

"Let me, Dad." I wet the styptic pencil and smoothed some on his chin. The bleeding stopped.

"Beth, as soon as I get my head straight, we'll make arrangements. You've been great about your grandmother."

"I'm trying, but she's really bugging me."

"Hang in just a little longer and we'll all sit down and have a talk and get straightened out."

"She's on my back over every little thing, Dad. She acts as if I have to report in and out every time I go to the bathroom. Mom . . ." I was proud of myself, I hardly even choked on the word. "My God, Mom and you always let me come and go as I pleased."

"I know, baby." His hand reached out to my hair again and this time the warmth of the small bathroom and the sweet overpowering smell of the Aramis and the gentle touch were too much for me. I turned and left the room.

When he finished dressing, we walked down to Grandma's apartment.

"Beth." I was enveloped by Aunt Nina. She took my face between her hands. "You look fantastic." She found the same loose hair Dad had, only her touch was a little more critical. "But we've got to do something about that hair. Maybe next week you can meet me in the city. I'll take you to Pablo. He owes me about three hundred favors."

"Hi, Nina." Dad reached across me and kissed Aunt Nina on the cheek. I don't think they had spoken since the last night of Shiva.

"Hi, Steve," Aunt Nina answered lightly. "As handsome as ever, I see."

"And the famous model is still as gorgeous as ever, though her mascara is smeared a little bit."

"Where?" Aunt Nina put her hand to her cheek. Then she caught Dad's teasing smile. "Oh, fine, I should know better than to listen to you."

"On the contrary, someone who earns sixty bucks an hour with her face should be happy to have a brother-in-law take an interest in it."

"Sit, everybody. Sit. Dinner is ready." Grandma was wiping her hands on one of her big flowered aprons. I was sorry she interrupted. I loved to hear Dad and Aunt Nina tease each other.

There was an awkward moment before we sat down. The table seemed immense. Amazing that one slim lady had so filled a room.

The Sabbath candles were glowing. Grandma had lit them at sundown. They stood in the middle of the table: two brass candlesticks, one listing slightly to the left. They had been in the family for years. Grandma's mother had brought them with her from the old country. They fascinated me when I was little. I pictured a scene from *Fiddler on the Roof*, where all the daughters in the family stood around the Sabbath candles in their peasant dresses and kerchiefed heads on a swept mud floor.

Mother had a pair of Lenox china candlesticks that she lit every Sabbath. The brass sticks were supposed to have become Mother's after Grandma's death. Last week Grandma repromised them to me, because she didn't think Aunt Nina would ever get married. So there they were, lighting the Sabbath. I wondered if the brass candlesticks knew they would skip a whole generation when they settled in their next home.

"Well, let's begin. Steve, I poured the wine, please say Kiddush." Daddy winked at me, but he stood up and raised the wine glass to say the blessing that would begin our meal.

"Wait, wait a minute. No prayer without a yarmulke." Grandma ran into the kitchen.

Daddy put his hand over his head. "Sit down, Mom. Look, I'm covering my head."

"No, no. You must wear a yarmulke for the blessing." Aunt Nina and I laughed. This too was a ritual that went on weekly—Daddy trying to get the blessing in before Grandma made him put on the yarmulke. He blessed the wine and then blessed the Sabbath challah and we were ready to eat.

We passed the wine cup and each took a sip from it. Then Dad passed pieces from the first cut of challah. Grandma started to cry when the cup reached her and we all looked away.

"Well, Nina, what brings you home tonight?" Daddy began the conversation.

"You'll never believe it." Aunt Nina was smiling her regular smile, not her camera smile, so I knew it must be something exciting.

"From you, I'll believe it. How long are you going to be home this time?"

Aunt Nina sat back in her chair. "I would say about two weeks."

"Two weeks?" Even Grandma Bernstein was surprised.

"Two weeks?" Daddy laughed again. "Did they find another face to use for Darling products or are you giving all the bachelors in New York time off?"

"Very funny." Aunt Nina pushed away a plate of gefilte fish. "No, no more, Ma, you know I can only eat one piece."

"Hmm." Grandma sniffed. "I cook all day and one piece is all you eat."

"Nobody told you to cook all day. Gefilte fish come in jars too, you know."

Grandma looked as if someone had told her that Moshe Dayan was an Arab spy. "Gefilte fish in a jar. Never in my house. Over my dead body you'll eat gefilte fish in a jar."

Again that sudden stillness in the air. Would it always be like this? Everyday expressions hung in the air over the overwhelming fact of my mother's death.

Daddy broke the silence. He looked good tonight. He still had circles under his eyes—we all did—and I saw a lot more of his hair curling over the top of his white shirt, and his sideburns were a little too thick. Dad's eyes are gray, real gray, and he has these long tangly eyelashes that Mother and I used to sigh for. Even Aunt Nina has said she would trade the dimples on her shoulder for Dad's eyelashes. I guess I would have to say that my father is a handsome man.

"Well, Nina, come tell us. What brings you home to the bosom of your family for two weeks?" He was teasing again.

Aunt Nina put her fork down. She leaned her elbows on the table and posed with her hands crossed under her face. It's very hard for Aunt Nina to talk without posing. I guess that's the way you get when you're constantly looked at.

"Well, dear family, Nina Frankle has finally landed a TV commercial."

Even Grandma Bernstein put her fork down. I forgot to chew the rest of my fish. Aunt Nina was all over the magazines but she had been dying to break into TV.

"Oh, Aunt Nina, fantastic! What for? Shampoo! It must be that shampoo commercial."

She swung her fabulous auburn hair gently, signaling no.

Daddy paused between bites of fish. "Nails. They have a new color called Pago Pago Pink and they're sending you to Pago Pago to sit on a volcano in a sarong and hand a mango to a gorilla while showing off your nails."

Even Grandma began to laugh. "This horseradish is too strong tonight. Come, Nina, tell us what it is."

Aunt Nina put both hands on the table. "I have returned to grow hair on my legs."

"Hair on your legs?" Now I was puzzled.

"Would you believe that Darling is putting a new depilatory on the market and I landed the job of showing how to use it?"

Daddy reached for another piece of challah. "They're going to shave your legs on TV?"

"No, no, Steve. You will see me taking a shower." She turned to Grandma who had her mouth open indignantly.

"Don't worry, Ma, all you're going to see are my legs—hairy legs. Then I step out of the shower and sit down on a chair—and smooth on the hair-removing cream—and *voilà!* In a few seconds wipe it off and my skin will be baby smooth."

"But, Aunt Nina, why do you have to grow it first?"

"Because TV commercials are supposed to be one-hundred-percent accurate nowadays. Therefore it must be my hair on my legs that must be removed by me in front of the cameras."

Grandma started to clear the fish dishes away. "*Meshugah*. Last week you paid sixty dollars to a beauty parlor to have your legs waxed clean. Now you're going to grow it back?"

"Believe it! Not only am I going to get paid, and very well paid, for the commercial but I am also going to get paid for the two weeks it takes me to grow the hair back on my legs."

"Beth, help me bring in the soup. *Meshugah!* Getting paid to grow hair."

Daddy and Aunt Nina were laughing together as I helped Grandma serve the soup. It was steaming hot. Chicken soup with matzoh balls—my absolute favorite. Grandma's soup was very thick and she never strained it, so you always caught pieces of carrots and parsley and dill between your teeth. Globules of fat swam on top. You could put your spoon in the middle and try to break them up. They would separate like amoeba cells under a microscope and then rejoin to form another big circle of fat. I closed my eyes as I bit into a matzoh ball. The outside was very soft and almost crumbled as you ate it, but the inside was hard and very chewy. There is something to all the jokes about chicken soup. It does make you feel better when you eat it. Even Joyce loves chicken soup when she's sick and her mother's soup comes from a bouillon cube.

Grandma's soup was the real McCoy. No one talked while we ate the soup, and even Aunt Nina never mentioned how many calories she was consuming. I got a lump in my throat and it wasn't from the matzoh ball or the steaming liquid. It was the memories of all the holidays and Sabbath dinners past and those that were yet to come that stuck in my throat.

When we were finished with dinner, Aunt Nina and I stacked the dishes in the dishwasher. Grandma bustled around us. "Rinse. Rinse off first, Beth."

"Grandma, what's the sense of having a dishwasher if you don't wash dishes in it?"

"Never you mind. Here, give me that plate." Aunt Nina raised her eyebrows behind Grandma's back. I raised mine back as another memory filtered through the air between us—a memory of two sisters. Was I taking Mother's place?

Grandma handed back the plate. It was gleaming. Aunt Nina ran a thumbnail across it. "You did it again, Ma, squeaky clean." I reached up to put it away in the cupboard. Grandma stopped me.

"In the dishwasher, Beth, in the dishwasher."

"But, Grandma, you got it cleaner than the dishwasher would."

Aunt Nina laughed. "Ma, I got you this dishwasher to save the aggravation of washing dishes."

"I use it. The hot water kills the germs. Put the plate in the dishwasher."

Dad poked his head into the kitchen. "Beth, telephone for you."

Aunt Nina called out, "Male or female?"

"I believe male. From the sound of his voice I would say he's about five-feet, eight-inches, with red hair tied in a pony-tail and a tiny Dachshund that's barking in the background."

"Whew." Aunt Nina wiped her brow simulating relief. "Thank goodness it's for you, Beth."

"Oh, Daddy." I ran to the phone laughing.

Dad called out, "Ask him if he has a five-foot, five-inch, bald, bearded brother with a Great Dane for your aunt!"

For the first time in a month, I answered the phone with a "hi" that I really meant. It was Kenny.

"Hi yourself."

And for the first time in a month, I leaned back against Grandma's couch, tucked my knees up, and let Kenny's voice warm me.

"Beth . . ."

"Yeah, Ken."

I always told Joyce that Kenny's voice on the telephone could untangle the extension cord.

"I *am* going to see you tomorrow, right?"

"Right."

"I'll just honk the horn, OK?" He paused. "It's just that I know your grandmother isn't too crazy about me."

"That's OK, Ken. Just honk."

"OK, tomorrow."

"Yeah, tomorrow. And, Kenny, good luck tonight. Score a hundred."

"Don't I wish. I'll settle for sixteen." Even though he hadn't won a scholarship to college, Kenny was trying to break Millburn's individual scoring record. Again, he wouldn't talk much about it but I knew he only needed thirty more points and he had a half-dozen games left to do it in. I hoped to be there the night it happened.

"Tomorrow, Beth. Take care."

I hung up the phone and stretched. Kenny's voice untangled extension cords, but it curled toes.

Aunt Nina and Grandma walked into the room. They had their coats on. Daddy followed.

"C'mon, Beth, put your coat on. We'll be late for services." Daddy held my coat out for me.

I waited for a moment, looking past the three of them into the darkened kitchen. And then I realized that we were all in the living room. The person I was waiting for was not going to walk into the room and join us.

I reached for my coat, my toes no longer curling. It was time to go say Kaddish for my dead mother.

Six

We can walk to our synagogue. It's Conservative, which means that the men and women sit together. My grandmother had trouble getting used to this at first. She had only attended Orthodox services.

When I was a little girl and Grandpa Lou was alive, we all went to services at his synagogue. We would walk in the front door together, but then we separated. The men went into the main part of the sanctuary. The women sat behind a Mehitzah, which is a separating wall built down the center of a synagogue. It sounds worse than it was. In some Orthodox synagogues the women sit upstairs, separated from the men by a balcony.

I would stay very close to Mother. She always tried to get me a seat near the partition. The bottom half was made of wood and the top had a thick curtain covering it. You couldn't see in or out. The women would sit with their prayer books open and pray very loudly, moving their lips and sometimes moaning and sobbing. Mother would show me a book. I would watch her finger trace the thick black letters that covered the page and wonder if I would ever be able to read this strange Hebrew language.

Mother and Grandma followed the service closely. You could hear the rabbi's voice coming over the curtain. Aunt Nina hardly ever went with us, and when she did go, there would always be a fight. She would sit still for about five minutes and then whisper loudly, "Ma, I'm going. I'll see you home."

Grandma would try to argue, but Aunt Nina would walk out. Sometimes I would ask Mother if I could go with Aunt Nina, but she would say, "Just try to sit for another five minutes, Beth."

Mother always brought lifesavers in her pocketbook and that would keep me busy for a while. She also had a special charm bracelet that she wore on holidays. It was a mixture of pearls and gold. There were three charms. When I really got restless, Mother would let me wear the charm bracelet. One charm was a large gold heart, trimmed with pearls. Inside was a picture of Mother and Daddy in their wedding finery. Daddy had this big pompadour hairdo and no sideburns. He was wearing a top hat and it was tipped slightly to the side so that his ears looked as if they were sticking out. Mother had a soft smile, her page boy hairdo, and a crown of orange blossoms. You could see the white veil behind both of them like a filmy cloud. The date was engraved on the back of the heart—"Janet and Steve, October 23, 1959."

The next charm was a large circle of gold with the number 30 outlined in pearls. It was engraved, "To Janet, on her 30th.

Love, Steve." And the last charm was a gold disk with a baby's shoe, a baby's bottle, and a small teething ring. It too was inscribed: "Beth, April 9, 1961."

After I got tired of looking at the charm bracelet and sucking lifesavers I would wonder what was going on behind the curtain. Daddy had taken me into the main sanctuary many times, when there were no services going on. I had seen the seats surrounding the Bimah, or platform where the rabbi and cantor stand and the Holy Ark that holds the Torahs, or Five Books of Moses. But I was convinced that something very unusual must go on during services, otherwise they wouldn't separate us this way.

I would try to wait for a moment when no one was looking to peek under the curtain. But the old ladies were very watchful. You would think their eyes were right on the prayer book. They would be rocking back and forth and POW—the minute I would lift a corner of the curtain, a voice would hiss, "No, no, *mein Kindt,* don't do that."

One holiday they all seemed to be occupied. Those who weren't studying their prayer books were engaged in a conversation about Mrs. Levy's new mink stole. I peeked under the curtain. At first I was very disappointed. There were just rows and rows of men, sitting in their yarmulkes and talaysim or prayer shawls, and praying in their books, the same way the ladies were doing. But suddenly one of them got up to say a special prayer. I think it must have been on Rosh Hoshanah or Yom Kippur, the Day of Repentance. The man's prayer shawl was not just a narrow strip that went around the neck. He was wrapped up in a large triangle of cloth. It was around his head, over his yarmulke, and draped his shoulders and arms. Then he spread his arms to the side and cried out to the Ark in front of him. The huge prayer shawl spread out behind him like gigantic wings. As he stood there swaying in prayer, with the shawl in constant motion, I thought he looked like an enormous bird ready to take flight and petition God in person. I let go of the curtain. Of course, the men were engaged in some mystical formula that would help them fly right up to Heaven in person and the partition was to keep all the ladies from finding out the formula. Maybe Mother was now in on the secret.

Daddy gave me a poke with his elbow at the same time that Rabbi Morton was pounding on his lectern trying to make a point with his fists that he was unable to make with his words. It sounded as if his sermon were almost over, though you never could tell. One of his degrees must have been in theater arts, because he delivered his sermons with all the ruffles and flourishes his voice was capable of and all the movement that the restrictions of the lectern would allow.

Finally, he was finished. No, just as he turned away, he strode dramatically back to pound out another point and wake the rest of the sleepers. Daddy nudged me again and I gave a little giggle. He and I were kindred spirits when it came to Rabbi Morton's sermons.

Before the very end of the service, it was the custom in our synagogue for everyone in mourning to rise and say Kaddish, the prayer for the dead. Daddy and I rose with Grandma. Aunt Nina sat very still until Grandma's pinch made her stand up too. I tried to look straight ahead as I said the prayer. I looked at the Ark and the Ner Tamid, or "Eternal Light," that was hanging in front of it. It was always supposed to be lit—a sign that God was watching over his people or something like that.

The Eternal Light in our synagogue hung from a goldlike chain and looked like a large lantern covered with grillwork. The light flickered inside. In ancient times it was supposed to be lit with pure olive oil, but today I guess gas or electricity is used. As we said the prayer I felt exposed. Eyes on me from the back and the sides of the congregation. Eyes that were stripping my clothes and my skin, leaving nothing but my very skeleton to hold me up. I know I wasn't imagining the eyes. On past Friday nights, I had stared at the people saying Kaddish. Stared and shivered to myself—a happy shiver wondering how they could bear it, and thanking God that I wasn't saying the prayer for the dead. Well, now I was a bona fide mourner.

The prayer ended and we sat down. I felt Daddy's strength next to me and I relaxed against the back of my seat. As I continued to stare at the Ner Tamid, it seemed as if the light had gone out. No, it was just the flickering of the flame. But a shadow crossed my father's body and I felt the icy shiver that had begun when I learned about Mother's death. Daddy was strong, so healthy. But Mother had been too. And look where she was now. I forced myself to take a deep breath and followed my family out of the pews.

Aunt Nina wanted to go right home. "C'mon, Ma," she said, "I've used up my quota of religion for the next ten years." Grandma wanted to stay for the traditional refreshments that followed Friday night services. I didn't care. My night was ruined anyway. It was too late to go to the basketball game.

We sat down at one of the long white-clothed tables with other members of the congregation. The ladies from the synagogue sisterhood had set out trays of tiny cookies and pastries and were busy pouring tea. I had some tea but didn't touch the pastries. They reminded me of all the boxes that had been brought to our house while we were sitting Shiva.

Lots of friends of my father and mother came up to shake hands and wish us well. There weren't too many kids my age around. Joyce, like most of my other friends, was at the basketball game. Where I would have been, if . . .

Rabbi Morton leaned down to talk to Grandma and she started to cry. Boy, for a guy with all his degrees he didn't know when to stop. Mrs. Benson was pouring tea at the other end of the table. She saw Grandma and put down her teapot. "Excuse me, Rabbi Morton," she said. "Come with me, Mrs. Bernstein, I want to show you the new teacups the sisterhood bought. They haven't been unpacked yet."

Still crying, Grandma let herself be led away to the kitchen. "That was nice of Anita," said Dad.

"Huh!" snorted Aunt Nina. "You know who she'd *really* like to take for a walk, and I don't mean to the kitchen."

I hoped Aunt Nina didn't mean what I thought she did. "She was just being nice, Aunt Nin." I never could figure out how someone as beautiful as Aunt Nina could get so nasty at times. I'd be the happiest person in the world if I looked like her. Then I'd be sure about Kenny.

Mrs. Benson returned with Grandma. The tears had stopped. They both sat down and Mrs. Benson poured tea for herself and Grandma.

She spoke to Aunt Nina. "How are you, Nina? You look great, and as usual I can't pick up a magazine without seeing your picture."

Aunt Nina smiled over the coffee cup. It was her in-front-of-the-camera smile, not her real one. Aunt Nina always said she hated women, that she never had any close girl friends. Aunt Nina always said that my mother was the only woman she had ever trusted.

Mrs. Benson continued. "And that suede suit you have on. It's gorgeous. I've been dying for one just like it."

Aunt Nina didn't even look down to check her suit. "It's Halston. He insisted that I keep it after I modeled it in a charity show."

"I should have known. A Halston. And that color—you do look fabulous. You know we wanted to have a fashion show here at the synagogue to raise some money for new seats."

Aunt Nina didn't let her finish. "I'm sorry, Anita, but I'm completely booked for the rest of the year."

"Well, maybe some of your friends who aren't busy would donate their time. It's for charity."

"Sorry, I don't mix my professional life with my personal life."

Mrs. Benson smoothed down her bangs and patted the side of her hair. You could tell she didn't know what to say next. I had to hand it to her though. She took a big sip of tea and turned to Daddy. "I'd like to send some literature out to you, Steve."

"Literature?" Daddy looked puzzled. His hands covered the blue porcelain teacup. I wanted to warn him to be careful, there was a tiny crack on the outer edge. The sisterhood should have unpacked the new cups. My mother had been on the committee that picked them out. I guess that even though Mother didn't have a professional life, she mixed her personal life with other things when people asked her.

Mrs. Benson was still fussing with a piece of bang that

wouldn't lay flat and glancing at Aunt Nina. Women always started fussing with themselves when Aunt Nina was around. She was so perfect looking, she could make you feel that your slip was showing or you had a big pimple on your face even when you didn't.

"When you were sitting Shiva, remember, I told you that when you were ready I'd send you some literature about meetings and things."

Daddy looked as if he were having trouble remembering the conversation. That whole week was one great blur to us. He put the cup down. At home he drank coffee, hot and black, in a large brown pottery mug that said "Dad" and had a hand-painted mustache in the middle. Mother had a matching mug that said "Mom" and had a hand-painted rolling pin in the center. We had bought them at a fair in the Amish part of Pennsylvania.

Mrs. Benson squeezed my shoulder as if to include me in the conversation. "Our meetings, you remember. Parents Without Partners. It's really a rap group, but we get together and socialize, take trips, go out to dinner, have wine and cheese parties. You know, that sort of thing. We're all in the same boat and it does you good to talk to someone with the same problems."

Parents Without Partners—I didn't get it. I looked at Aunt Nina. She had her hands folded underneath her chin and was staring at Daddy as if to say, I told you so.

Grandma joined the conversation. "Steve has a lot to do, Anita, without running around to meetings. He has a home and a daughter." Grandma smoothed back my hair.

It was wonderful the way I was trotted out whenever somebody needed an excuse for something.

"Well, Anita, it was very nice of you to think of me." Daddy stood up and shook Mrs. Benson's hand. "But right now"—he stopped for a minute—"right now, Beth and I have a lot to do to straighten out our everyday lives and get things back together the best we can."

Mrs. Benson leaned forward. Ever since she had sat down I had been trying to figure out what her perfume smelled like. Lilacs—the huge purple hanging ones. "Oh, Steve, that's exactly what I mean. That's how Parents Without Partners can help you. We've all gone through what you're going through. I'd be happy to go with you to the first couple of meetings. I know how it feels to walk in someplace alone."

I guess I had known what Mrs. Benson was up to from the moment she had come around. I just didn't want to admit that Aunt Nina was right. Grandma was sitting there looking as if steam was going to come out of her ears any minute and Daddy wanted to leave. Parents Without Partners. Anita Benson, divorcée, and Steve Frankle. I looked at Daddy. My father's a handsome man and he doesn't have a wife anymore. Mrs. Benson's lilacs were really making me nauseous. That perfume just hung over her like a cloud. Mother's perfume used to dance ahead of her, clearing a path. You could smell Mother before she entered the room and long after she was gone, but gently.

Daddy moved toward the door. "Let's go, Beth." He nodded to Aunt Nina and held the chair for Grandma. "I've got to get my girls home. We're all tired."

"I'll mail you the stuff, Steve. Then you can look at it at your leisure."

We got our coats and walked out the door. Aunt Nina was the first to speak. "Ah, suburbia. Congratulations, dear brother-in-law, you have just been officially placed in the singles go-round by Anita Benson. By this time on Monday, every computer bank in the country will have your age, vital statistics, your last six golf scores, and whether you prefer blondes, brunettes, or bald eagles."

Grandma mumbled. "Indecent, that's what it is. Indecent. My Janet. Only gone a month and already it's starting."

Now that we were away from the smell of lilacs I felt better. Maybe Aunt Nina and Grandma were overreacting. Mrs. Benson had looked pretty lonely herself when we walked out. Besides, Daddy wouldn't get involved with any dumb group like that. Mrs. Benson had two little kids; she probably needed the company. But Daddy had me. "You know, Aunt Nina, she's not so bad. She practically cracked up after her divorce. Mom used to say that all she needed was another man."

Aunt Nina pulled the back of my hair. "That's exactly what I mean." Grandma was still mumbling under her breath.

Daddy put his arm around her. "Come on, Ma. She was just trying to be friendly. And, Nina, quit worrying about me. You've got two weeks to concentrate on growing your hair. This is one commercial I'm going to be happy to watch."

Daddy and his harem. He used to call us that when Mother was alive and he'd take us all out to eat or to a movie. He reached out for me and I snuggled under his arm. He held me close and I tried to match my stride to his.

When I was little it had taken two long strides and one short hop to keep up with his long legs, and when we came to a curb he would put his hand under my armpits and swing me over to the other side.

"Hey, Beth."

"Yes, Dad." I watched our breath curl together and float skyward in the cool night air.

"Tomorrow's Saturday night. Right? Right! How about you and me taking off and we'll do the city?"

"Do the city!" He and Mother used to "do the city" on Saturday night. "We'll eat dinner," he went on, "and I'll try to pick up tickets to a show or movie. Anything in particular you'd like to see? Maybe just a leisurely dinner. Say, I've got it. Windows on the World—the new spot on top of the World Trade Center. Mother and I were going to take you there. How about it? You can see all of New York, New Jersey, and part of Connecticut. Hey, look at that sky!"

He took my hand in his and Grandma's hand on the other side. "Grab hold, Nina." Aunt Nina skipped to take Grandma's other hand. Daddy's voice was booming. "What's that you used to say about stars when you were little, Beth? Star light, star bright, first star . . ."

"*Meshugah!*" But Grandma's voice was very loving as she said it again. "*Meshugah!*"

Aunt Nina joined her voice to Daddy's. ". . . I've seen tonight . . ."

Daddy squeezed my hand. He needed me, not Parents Without Partners. What should I wear to New York tomorrow night? I'd better ask Aunt Nina how dressy they get at this restaurant.

Daddy gave me a little shove. "Come on, Beth . . . wish I may, wish I might . . ."

I joined in as we reached the corner. I stumbled over the curbstone. Tomorrow was Saturday. Kenny had been waiting for a month. What was I going to tell him?

Seven

Dad went to the golf course in the morning. He usually did on Saturdays, even when it got so cold that he had to wear gloves and a knitted hat pulled over his head. Once, for Father's Day, Mother and I bought a box of golf balls and painted them red and blue. Mother wrote a poem. She was always good at that. I still remember it.

"When Jack Frost comes, and cold winds blow . . .
You'll spot these balls, through all that snow!"

I got out of bed quickly. Joyce was coming over. We had to work on a report for school, and I had to call Kenny about tonight. I shivered. Grandma must have turned down the thermostats again. Each apartment had its own heat control, but now that Grandma wandered in and out of our place all the time, she kept setting our thermostat lower than we usually kept it.

Last week I told her I was freezing.

"Freezing," she answered. "You should have been on the East Side when I came to America. Then you could talk about freezing."

Oops, I had said the magic words again. Grandma was like a computer. Anytime you fed her a complaint about being warm or cold, hungry or full, she was programmed to spit back statistics on how fortunate you were compared to what she had gone through.

"We used to save newspapers just to push into the spaces in the wall that the wind came through. And we used to wrap newspapers around our legs when we walked outside. And we used cardboard on the inside of our shoes when the soles were worn and there was no money for new shoes . . ."

When Grandma talked like that, I felt guilty about throwing newspapers away. She always stored hers in the basement and gave them away when charities held paper drives.

There was a knock on the door. I didn't bother with a robe. Joyce always ran up the steps and knocked. Anybody else would have rung the bell.

"Hi, Beth—you still in your pajamas?"

"Yeah, we got home late last night from temple. Now if you were a good Jewish girl you would have been there instead of at the basketball game. Who won anyway?"

"Are you kidding? They'd have to drag me there with a derrick to listen to Rabbi Morton. We won 94–72."

"Oh, Rabbi Morton was terrific last night."

"He was? What did he talk about?"

"I haven't the faintest idea and neither did he, but it was a nice sermon to nap to. I wouldn't have gone either if, well . . . you know, it was the last night . . ."

Joyce interrupted. "You don't have to explain. I know the month is over. Now you can start going out with us again on Friday nights. There's still half of basketball season left."

Basketball season! Kenny! He was the last person I had thought about last night. I still had to call him. Joyce followed me into my room as I threw on jeans and a shirt. As I dressed, I told her about going out with my father.

"So what do you think I should tell Kenny, Joyce?"

"Do you have to go with your father?"

"Joyce!" I put down my toothbrush and glared at her. I still had a mouthful of toothpaste. How could she even think I would go out with Kenny when my father needed me?

"OK, OK. Don't get so mad. And please spit, you look like a foaming dog."

"What should I tell him?"

"Tell him the truth. But couldn't you go with your father during the week?"

"No, Joyce." The towel fell off the rack. I tried to smooth it out as I put it back. "I told you we're going to Windows on the World."

"Yeah, you told me." Joyce shrugged.

I could tell by her attitude that she didn't think it was so great to be going out with my father instead of Kenny.

"I'm going to call him right now." I don't know why I was so nervous. This was Kenny, he'd understand. Hadn't he just told me the other day to take my time with things? I mean, we weren't just going together because of sex or something.

I dialed the number. I made Joyce stand next to me and held onto her fingers with my empty hand. After all these months I still couldn't believe that Kenny Perna had picked me to go around with. My mother always told me I didn't have enough confidence in myself, that I was just as attractive as any of the other girls. I guess I still can't help worrying that Kenny may drop me as easily as he picked me.

"Hello, Mrs. Perna, is Kenny home? . . . It's Beth Frankle." I held my hand over the mouthpiece and whispered to Joyce, "She's such a pain. She always says, 'Who's calling please?' She knows damn well it's me."

Joyce covered a giggle. "Why don't you surprise her once and tell her you're a famous TV star who has fallen madly in love with her son the basketball player?"

Now she had me giggling. "Shut up, Joyce, here he is."

"Ken? It's me. How many points?"

Kenny must have just gotten up. He still had sleep in his voice. "Fourteen. I missed two free throws, though."

"Fourteen. Oh, I wish I'd been there!"

"Yeah, you should have been. What's up? How come you're calling so early anyway, something wrong?"

"No, no, everything's fine. It's just about tonight, Kenny."

He yawned. "What about tonight?"

I closed my eyes tight and got the sentence out as quickly as I could. "Kenny, about tonight, I know we had a special date and—I-feel-terrible-about-it, but I just have to go someplace with my father."

There was a pause. Joyce was moving her lips. "What's he saying? What's he saying?" I shook my head at her to be quiet.

Then I heard Kenny's voice again. "Where do you have to go with your father, to visit relatives or something?"

"Not exactly. Look, Kenny, my father is feeling really lousy and we're going out to eat together."

"What time will you be home?"

"That's just it. We're going to New York and won't be home until late, so I won't be able to see you tonight."

His voice didn't change. "OK, Beth, that's cool. See you around." The phone clicked.

"What did he say?" Joyce had curled up on the sofa. Sometimes words hurt more than a punch in the stomach and I had to wait a minute to catch my breath.

"Nothing. Just nothing." I slammed the receiver down.

"Oh, come on, you should know Kenny already. He'll be calling you back in an hour to apologize."

"If that's the way he's going to be, he can just apologize to himself. I mean, my mother just died and I'm going spend the evening with my father and I have to make excuses to Kenny Perna?"

"Oh, come on, Beth. Don't be upset." She waved her arms in the air. "Some day you'll look back on all this when you and Kenny are married and have eighty-eight children and laugh."

She was using her movie-star English accent.

I threw a pillow at her. "Just what I always wanted— eighty-eight children!" But she had me laughing.

Joyce tossed me a book. "I think we'd better start on this stupid thing if we're ever going to finish it."

I grabbed my notebook. Back to lovely medieval England . . . "The Wars of the Roses"—I titled my page with firm black letters. "Do you really think I'll end up with Kenny, Joyce?"

She took the pencil out of her mouth. "Of course, darling, it was written in the stars."

Later that day I went downstairs to check with Aunt Nina. She was lying on the couch reading. "How's the hair growing, Aunt Nin?"

She lifted her long robe and rubbed her fingers over her legs. "Stubble. Stage one. Looks as if I'm going to need the whole two weeks."

We discussed what I should wear and Aunt Nina said that my black velvet pants would be fine. There was a matching blazer jacket and a pale blue silk blouse. The outfit was from last year. I had only worn it once to a family wedding.

"Don't you have a date tonight, Aunt Nina?"

"Beth, love, I always have a date. But am I keeping it and going out? No."

"Are you still seeing David, Aunt Nin?"

Aunt Nina closed the book firmly. David Ramsey was a stockbroker and gorgeous enough to be a TV star himself. She had been seeing him about five months, which was a record for Aunt Nina. We hadn't met him, of course—just seen pictures. But Mother had told me she thought Aunt Nina was really in love this time.

"I'm seeing David Ramsey and I'm seeing Michael Webster and Paul Montgomery."

"Gee, Aunt Nina, how do you juggle them all?"

"Oh, it's a little trick I learned. It's called survival of the fittest."

I didn't get it and told her so.

"You will, honey. One day you will."

I told her what happened with Kenny.

"See?" Aunt Nina opened and closed her mouth widely a few times. "To quote your grandmother, which I never do, you put all your eggs in one basket." Aunt Nina continued to open her mouth as wide as she could and close it tightly.

"Aunt Nina, what are you doing with your mouth?"

"Exercises." She pointed to her neck. "It keeps the neck toned, so it doesn't get flabby."

"I'll have to remember that."

Then she stretched her neck as hard as she could backwards. Sometimes I think Aunt Nina has trained harder at staying beautiful than Ken has for the basketball team. Kenny!

"Yeah, Aunt Nina, but I don't want to see anyone else but Kenny."

"That too shall pass." With a sign of exhaustion, she stretched back on the couch.

"But look at Mom and Dad. Mom settled for one man. She was happy."

Aunt Nina picked up her book. For once she forgot to hold her face together. I could see it drop. And she had dark shadows under her eyes.

"Beth." Her voice sounded tired, as if she could hardly push words out of her mouth. "Your mother was a very special person and I wish to God she were here right now, so I could ask her what to do about David Ramsey."

I turned to go back upstairs.

"And, Beth"—her voice had remembered who she was—"violet eye shadow tonight with that blue blouse. Don't put blue on. Strictly Hicksville to match eye color with your clothes."

"OK, Aunt Nin."

She called out once more as I shut the door, "Remember, violet or mauve—don't wear blue!"

Eight

It seemed strange sitting in the car with my father, the two of us, all dressed up, going into the city. Sure, we had been alone lots of times, but now we knew that no one was waiting at home for us.

"Do you want some music, Beth?" We both reached for the radio switch and pulled away as our hands brushed together. Music! Anything would be better than the quiet that seemed to push me back against the car seat.

He tried again. "OK, Beth, we haven't had much time to talk. Tell me what's doing in school."

I guess WABC wasn't going to save me from the silence. What did I talk about in the days when I had a mother and we all drove in the car together and finally she and Dad would laugh and turn on the radio to stop me from talking?

He'd said "school"—so I started. Down the turnpike, through the Holland Tunnel, I talked: about the election for junior class president, about the report Joyce and I were doing for history on the Wars of the Roses, about how it was time to start writing for college catalogs, and about how boring gym class was.

Mother always had to yell, "Steve, watch the road!" because Dad would get involved in conversations and would talk with his hands and look over his shoulder to see if I was listening.

I didn't tell him that I had broken a date with Kenny. Dad wanted us to have this Saturday night on the town.

His eyes never left the road and the only time he took his hands off the wheel was to reach for a coin to throw in the toll box.

He asked about chemistry. Didn't he remember I had dropped it at the beginning of the term for an extra year of Spanish? I told him the scores of the last five basketball games and how Millburn would be county champs if we beat South Orange again. I felt if I stopped talking, we would both fall into a spinning vacuum and the car would ride on forever.

It was better when we got to the World Trade Center. We laughed going into the parking lot, past the automatic doors that open as a car enters.

"Hey, Dad, what happens if the door falls down on the middle of the car?"

"Let's hope it clears the front seat!"

There was a big crowd waiting in line in front of the elevators. Plush chains with gold links—the kind they use in movie theaters—held everyone in place. There were lots of couples on dates, the girls all dressed up in long skirts with high boots or smart pantsuits. I was glad I had listened to Aunt Nina. There was laughter and good-natured pushing in the line every time an elevator opened and a little bit of the crowd was allowed up.

The entrance hall was tremendous, with mirrored elevators and mirrored ceilings. When I was little and being taken to an exciting place, Aunt Nina would always say, "Don't stare, Beth, or point. You'll look like a hick." If all the people who were pointing and staring around me were hicks, then I guess the hicks have more fun than people like Aunt Nina who pretend to have seen everything.

I looked Dad over. He was perfect, as usual: pinstriped blue suit with a vest, white shirt, and a soft paisley tie. There was a line of people waiting behind a gold chain. From the looks of things we'd be standing a long time.

At the head of the line was a man dressed in a tux, holding a notebook. As we approached he held up his hand. "I'm sorry, sir, but unless you have a reservation there will be at least an hour's wait."

"I'm Mr. Frankle. I called during the week to reserve a table for two at eight o'clock."

The man checked the list. "Mr. Frankle. Here you are, sir. Go right up, please. And enjoy your dinner." He opened the chain, the next elevator arrived, and we were whisked inside. I heard people in the line protesting as the elevator doors shut. Visitors to New York sometimes don't realize how jammed restaurants are on Saturday nights. Dad must have been looking forward to this. As busy as he was in the office, he had remembered to make a reservation. I knew I had made the right decision in breaking my date with Kenny.

It was amazing, the elevator moved so quickly and silently that you could hardly feel it. One hundred and seven floors, nonstop. About halfway, I felt a popping in my ears. I turned to Dad.

He smiled. "Your ears popping?"

I nodded.

"Mine too. You don't realize how high up we are."

Other people complained of popping ears too. There was a lot of silly chatter. One girl called out, "Hey, I hope there are no mad bombers on this elevator."

Some of the ladies laughed, a little nervously, I thought.

"I just thought of something else!" It was the same girl. "What if the elevator gets stuck between floors?"

I unbuttoned my jacket. The elevator was closed in and smelled of perfume and after-shave and just plain people. I hoped I wasn't getting nauseated. Mother used to tell me that I talked myself into throwing up. She would make me take deep breaths or tell me a joke to get my mind off my stomach. Daddy's arms were folded across his chest and he stared straight ahead. I wondered what Kenny was doing.

The man with the loud girl spoke up. "Hey, Sherry, what do you want to frighten all these people for?"

"Me, frighten all these people?" Sherry giggled. "I thought of something else. What if this elevator just keeps going right up through the roof?"

It was no use taking deep breaths, there was no air in the elevator. Dad nudged me in the shoulder and bent close to my ear. "There's one in every crowd." As long as he remembered my weak stomach, I didn't need the deep breath.

When the elevator opened on the one-hundred-and-seventh floor we walked through more mirrored hallways. Our images were reflected and thrown back to us hundreds of times before we stepped up to a balcony and were in the restaurant proper.

"Oh, Daddy, look." I had to point.

So did he. "Over there, Beth, the bridges into Brooklyn."

"Daddy, the Statue of Liberty."

"Look, there's the New Jersey side. See that string of lights? I think it's the George Washington Bridge."

The maitre d' showed us to a table directly against one of the floor-length windows. The night was clear and it seemed as if the whole world were spread out for us. Millions of lights glittered on buildings and streets so tiny they looked as if they should be under a Christmas tree. Twinkling white lights moved on cars and buses with occasional green and red neon signs breaking through. You couldn't see the steel cables of the bridges, just their lights forming garlands and loops that trimmed the sky and ringed the city.

The Statue of Liberty stood at attention. She was guarding the city. From up here, she was a soft green and as I stared, her robes looked as if they were gracefully blowing in the wind, though the hand that held the welcome flare was very steady. I got a lump in my throat as I thought of Grandma coming to this country and running to the deck to get a look at Miss Liberty. Before I had always thought of the statue as a dirty monument which our fourth-grade class visited on a field trip.

Daddy was speaking to the waiter. "I'll have a Scotch on the rocks." He tapped my arm to bring me back into the room.

"Would you like something cold, Beth?"

I had two standbys in restaurants when everyone was having a drink: Coke or ginger ale. "Ginger ale, please." You have to be eighteen to have a drink in New York, but at least ginger ale looks like one.

"On the rocks too, please," I added.

The waiter smiled and gave us menus. "Very good." He moved off to the bar to get our drinks.

Daddy opened the menu. "The waiter's probably wondering what such a great-looking girl is doing with an old man."

"Oh, Daddy."

"No, I'm not kidding. I'll bet a lot of people looking at us probably think you're my girl friend, not my daughter."

We spent the next few minutes studying the tables around us. Daddy pointed out couples that he said were dates, even though the men were sometimes much older than the girls they were with. I was embarrassed but flattered that people would think I was my father's date instead of his daughter.

The drinks came. We clinked glasses in a toast.

"To us, Beth."

We clinked again. I guess I was supposed to say something. But the clink of the glasses reminded me of other toasts, other restaurants, where my mother would make everybody wait until the Coke I had ordered came and I could toast and clink my glass with everybody else. I think Daddy remembered too, because he put his glass down and leaned on his arm as he studied the outside.

I went back to the scenery too. It was like stepping outside of your body and into the sky. I sipped my drink. The longer you stared into it, the more you felt part of the night, twinkling with all those artificial lights. For a moment I put my hand on the window to make sure it was separating me from the outside. Daddy noticed.

"Planning on walking outside, Beth?"

"I don't know, Daddy. I suddenly got a feeling as if there were nothing between me and the sky."

We studied the menus. Daddy ordered some kind of rolled fish. I hesitated.

"Stop worrying about the price, Beth. I know you like steak. Order the sirloin."

Sometimes my father seems to be able to read my mind and at other times he acts as if I don't exist.

"You're just like your mother, a price reader. She always did that too. Wouldn't order something she liked because she thought it was too expensive. Always waited for other people to order first."

Daddy was on his second Scotch. His voice didn't have the fun in it anymore. "A lot of good it did her—being unselfish and good."

I held onto the stem of my glass. It was so narrow that if I squeezed any harder I would break it off.

Daddy reached for my hand. "Don't be like her, Beth. No, I don't mean that. I want you to be like her. She was everything that is good and kind and beautiful. What I mean is, take things too. Enjoy things." He got up suddenly. "I'll be right back."

I watched him go to the entrance and saw him disappear down the hallway. My stomach dropped. I saw a couple across from me staring. These tables were so close. All of a sudden I heard the chatter and noise around me. Words and phrases being tossed into the air by happy people on a night out. The room had a rhythm to it. With the band in the background providing the drumbeat, the noise would reach a loud crescendo, and then things would quiet down and you could hear the clink of forks, even the quiet click of ice cubes in glasses. I wondered if that couple had heard us talking.

My hands felt hot and sweaty. Daddy had probably gone to the men's room. What if he didn't come back? I had about three dollars with me. That was one of Grandma's rules. She called it "mad money," in case you got mad at your date and wanted to run away. Mother always called it security. "Just have a few dollars with you so you'll have a feeling of security, Beth."

I didn't need money tonight. I was with my father. He had been gone almost ten minutes now. Our dinners had arrived. The waiter came back. He pointed to my father's plate. "Is anything wrong, miss?"

"No. Yes. My father had to step out and make a phone call." I remembered my mother and put more authority in my voice. "Do you think you could keep that warm for him until he comes back?" The waiter whisked Dad's fish away. I cut my own lukewarm steak into pieces and watched the doorway.

There Dad was. He came over, leaned down and put his hands on my shoulders, and dropped a gentle kiss on the top of my head. He cleared his throat and took his seat. "Sorry, baby."

The knot in his tie was crooked, off center. As if it had been torn loose because it was choking him. He cleared his throat again. The top of his hair looked damp. A drop of water still clung to the edge of one sideburn. The window reflected and enlarged the sadness in his eyes and the shadows underneath.

He tried again. "Too much sky, you, me . . ." His voice

trailed off. My God, I didn't know where in this wide-open mirrored palace he had found a place to cry, but I knew that my father had been crying.

The waiter brought back the fish. My father regained his voice. "Ah, terrific looking. Thank you. And, Beth, how's your steak? Done right? Are you sure?" He looked anxiously at my plate, where I had pushed the pieces of meat from side to side.

He leaned toward me. "Hey, you know what? When I passed the elevator operator he asked me where I picked up the great-looking chick I was with."

"Oh, Daddy." He had had his private moment. Those tears belonged to him and my mother. Mine would have to find their own time.

"Oh, Daddy. You're too much!" I started to laugh. And cut my meat. And eat. The juices were flowing again.

Nine

Sunday started slowly. It was hard for me to get my head out of the covers. Daddy was already in the living room, the Sunday papers spread across the floor.

"Good morning, Dad. Oh, please don't lose the 'News of Week in Review'—I need it for history."

"Hi, sleepyhead. Can't take late hours? I was just ready to see if you needed resuscitation."

Sunday used to be lox-and-bagels day. Daddy would go out early to the stores and come home loaded with bagels, about four assorted cheeses, salty lox, and hot Danish pastries. Mother would scramble eggs, carefully scraping the lox out of the portion she served me. Sometimes Grandma would come upstairs—and Aunt Nina too, if she were home.

The tile in the kitchen was cold under my feet. There was half a cup of coffee on the table. One lonely spoon dripped some cream off the edge. I opened the refrigerator door.

Grandma had stocked up. There were oranges and sour cream and pot cheese and two quarts of milk and English muffins that looked cold and unappetizing in their cellophane wrapping. Well, I never eat breakfast anyway.

"Dad," I yelled. "Do you want me to make you something? We have some eggs. I can make grilled cheese on an English muffin."

"No, thanks," came the answer. "I had some coffee. But make yourself something."

There was a knock on the door. I heard Daddy talking to Grandma.

"No, of course we're up. Come on in, Mom."

"Listen." I heard Grandma's voice. You could always tell when she was nervous. Her accent got thicker.

"Listen," she repeated. "I don't have to barge in. I just made a nice noodle pudding for lunch and I thought you and Beth . . ." Her voice trailed off.

Thank God for garbage disposals. I had ground up more nice meat loaves and nice casseroles in the past month than I could count. I was afraid to throw them in the garbage because Grandma probably searched it to see whether we were eating properly.

She walked into the kitchen. "Beth, put slippers on. The floor is cold."

I had just been going for my slippers, but after Grandma told me to, I got stubborn. "I'm fine, Grandma."

She put the noodle pudding on the stove top and reached for a sponge from the sink. The coffee cup and spoon were rinsed clean and on the drain board, and the table was wiped dry before I could take a breath. She dug a finger into one of the hanging plants. "A little dry. Usually I water Monday, but I think it needs a little today."

"Gram, you don't have to do that. I can water the plants." She beat me to the little gold watering can.

Funny, with all her talking, Grandma had never said a word about the plants being torn up. I'm sure she knew something had happened. The ones over the sink were still scraggly and uneven. She worked her way round the kitchen, pouring just the right amount and wiping up any drippings with the sponge.

Daddy walked in as she finished. "Now I want the both of you for supper tonight. I'm making a nice big brisket. And Nina hardly eats a thing. Like a bird. No, even a bird eats. You can see bones right through her clothes."

"You're supposed to see her bones, Grandma. That's why she's such a good model, because of her bones."

"She's too thin. If you come to dinner, maybe she'll eat more."

"How's her hair growing? Is she ready to go back to work yet?" Daddy was smiling.

"You have to remind me yet of that nonsense. Every day a call from the agency. It's a wonder they don't send someone out to measure how long each hair is. How about if we eat around 5:30?"

"We'd love to, Ma, but I promised Beth Chinese food tonight."

We hadn't talked about Chinese food, but I was glad Daddy was thinking fast.

"Chinese food!" Grandma pursed her lips and looked at the ceiling as if she were begging forgiveness for the heathens in her family. People who keep kosher don't eat Chinese food.

Grandma never got used to the idea, or to the fact that Mother and Dad ate lobster and shrimp too.

Daddy put his arm around her. "Tell you what, why don't you put that brisket in the freezer and you and Nina come with us. I'll order you chicken chow mein. I promise you—no pork!"

Grandma slapped his hand away, but in fun. Daddy could always tease her out of a mood. "No, you don't. I've lived all my life without polluting my stomach with *trefe* food and I guess I can finish it the same way."

"What time is it? I have to call Joyce. She and I are finishing our report today."

"Invite her to go with us for supper. I'll drive her home afterward."

Grandma looked around the spotless kitchen. "If there's nothing for me to do, I'll go downstairs. Call if you need anything." She looked fragile all of a sudden. So little. Grandma always was tall and straight. Now she looked as crooked as her arthritic fingers.

"You know, Gram, I think you're right. It's cold in here. I'm going to put on slippers."

"That's good, Beth." She stood a little straighter as she reached the door. "I'll put half the brisket in the freezer so you'll have a decent meal tomorrow night."

Grandma shut the door. "She really means well, Beth. She's just lost without your mother." So softly that I almost missed it, he added, "like the rest of us."

Joyce came over at two and Daddy decided to go to the golf course for a couple of hours. We promised to be ready at six for dinner.

As soon as he left, Joyce pointed to the chair. "Sit down.

We've got to talk or I won't be able to work on the report."

"But listen, Joyce, I want your advice. Do you think I should call Kenny? He never called back yesterday. Of course, I was downstairs at my grandmother's, so maybe I missed him."

"That's what I want to talk about."

"You're so serious. You sound like a commercial where one best friend tells another about her bad breath."

"Believe me, right now, I'd rather tell you to go buy mouthwash."

"OK, Joyce, go." I pushed aside our notebooks and curled up on the couch.

"Well, I want to tell you before you hear from some other kids, but last night—well, Kenny sort of wound up with Marcie Gerard."

"Marcie Gerard!" My feet uncurled. "I don't believe it."

"It was really kind of like an accident."

"What do you mean? Was he with her or not?"

"Well, a whole bunch of kids were at the Maplewood flick and when we came out we saw Marcie and a couple of girls hanging around Kenny. Kenny asked us if we were going to the diner and we said yes, so he and Marcie met us there."

"You went with Kenny and Marcie? Kenny took Marcie, and you went with them?" I felt as if I had been slapped. Daddy and I had spent a nice evening, but Kenny had been in the back of my head practically the whole time. Neither he nor I had dated anybody else in months. Marcie Gerard had been after him from the day we stepped into high school. And Joyce was supposed to be my best friend. How could she go with them? I was boiling.

"How could you go with Kenny when he was with another girl?"

Joyce jumped up. "For God's sake, what was I supposed to do? Make a scene? I told you how it happened. It was nothing. We had some burgers at the diner and then he drove her home."

She paced back and forth in her stocking feet. She kicked one of her boots out of her path. "I mean, what could I do? Say, 'Kenny, what are you doing with Marcie?' I mean, what would you do if the situation were reversed? And after all, he was probably upset about your breaking the date to begin with."

"He was upset? He was upset?" Now I was pacing and screaming. I could feel my neck knot up. "He knows why I couldn't go out."

"Yeah. He knows. But what do you expect him to do? Join a Trappist monastery just because . . ."

"Go ahead. Finish the sentence. Join a monastery because my mother died."

Joyce slid on the polished floor. She caught herself on the arm of the couch. "Oh, come on, Beth, you know I didn't mean that. God, I don't want to hurt your feelings. It's just that Kenny's only human. He just wanted to have some fun."

"Well, what do you think I am? I'm human too." I really didn't want to cry, but the shrieking had let loose a bunch of things that had been caught in my throat. "I was out with my father, not another guy. And that's because my mother died a month ago. And my grandmother is on my back constantly, and can you see how lonely my father looks? And my boy-friend who's supposed to love me can't even wait to have fun without me, and my best friend who's supposed to love me goes with him! And now I suppose you'll tell me that's written in the stars too!" I ran into the bedroom and slammed the door, pulled a pillow over my head, and cried and cried. I think I must have used up all the moisture in my body, because I was finally left with dry sobs and eyes that felt hot and tight in their sockets.

After a while, there was a knock on the door. Joyce didn't wait for an answer. She walked over to the side of the bed.

"Go away." I was too hurt and embarrassed to turn around and look at her.

"Beth Frankle, if you don't turn around and drink this tea, I'm going to pour it on your head."

I turned over. She had a teacup balanced on the tray. A napkin folded like a fan was stuck in a glass. She pointed to it. "I couldn't find a rose. You're supposed to have a rose when you have a tray in bed." There were two Oreo cookies on the tray, along with a couple of Fig Newtons.

"Now sit up and drink."

"No, I don't want it."

"It's good for you."

"You sound like my grandmother."

"If you don't drink it, I'll call your grandmother."

I took the tray from her. I had a couple of more sniffs left in me.

"Your nose is all red." She handed me a tissue. "You look disgusting."

"Thanks a lot. You didn't boil the water enough. There's a white scum on top."

She scooped it off with the spoon. "I'm a sex symbol like

your Aunt Nina, not Betty Crocker. Now drink so we can talk."

"And you used a meat cup." In kosher homes, the meat and dairy dishes are kept separate.

"It's just tea. And tea you can put in anything. I know that much about my religion, dummy."

The phone rang. "Sit." Joyce paused in the doorway. "I'll get it for you."

"I don't want to talk to anyone. Unless it's Kenny. Or my father. Or sometimes Grandma calls instead of walking up . . ."

"I'm just going to say hello, not be your social secretary."

I drank the lukewarm tea and made a face. Betty Crocker had forgotten sugar. I heard Joyce on the phone.

"Just a minute, I'll ask her. Beth? Beth?"

"Who is it?"

"It's Mrs. Benson."

The teacup was shaking on the tray. Boy, wasn't this perfect timing?

"Tell her I'm taking a bath."

Joyce hung up the phone and came back in the bedroom. She had a message written on a piece of paper. "She said to remind your father that there is a wine-and-cheese-tasting get-together at the Y tonight at eight."

I grabbed the paper out of Joyce's hand and ripped it up. "Too bad I can't throw the pieces down the garbage disposal with the rest of the junk."

"What are you muttering about?"

، "Oh, Mrs. Benson, she's that blond divorcée who lives around the corner. You remember, I baby-sat for her a couple of times. She's after my father to join some sort of stupid group."

"She sounds OK. I mean, it was nice of her to invite your father to a party with people his own age."

"Nice! Can you picture my father sitting around in a room with a bunch of women who are looking for husbands?"

"He might like it." Joyce must have seen another storm warning appear on my face. "I mean, not all of them can be looking for husbands. And he'll probably start to go out with women. Maybe your Aunt Nina can fix him up with one of those gorgeous models." She really couldn't say anything right to me today. But she kept going. "I don't mean right away, but you know, maybe in a couple of months." She got busy smoothing the bedspread.

She was so wrong. Nobody realized how my father felt about my mother. I was tempted to tell her about his crying at Windows on the World. But there are some things you don't say to anybody, not even your best friend.

"Well, tonight he's taking us out for Chinese food, Joyce."

"Great. Now can we work on this report? The Wars of the Roses lasted one hundred years and we're taking as long to write this."

I took the tray into the kitchen. Joyce had our notebooks spread over the table. She was flipping through a reference book.

"Hey, Joyce?"

"What?"

"Was she hanging all over him?"

"Who?"

"Marcie Gerard!"

Ten

Kenny didn't call. It wasn't like him. Except for the week of Shiva, we always spoke to each other before we went to sleep. He didn't come along at the bus stop on Monday either. Joyce gave me a lecture as we rode to school. "This isn't the fifties. You didn't sign a lifetime contract not to go out with anyone else."

"Yeah, Joyce, but neither of us ever had."

"Well, so, he did. You've got equal time. Come to the Y dance next Saturday with me. They always have a fantastic group of guys from Columbia."

"But I don't want to go out with anyone else."

She sighed. "You're really Middle Ages. But I love you anyway." And she patted my shoulder.

I decided to wait near his locker. Maybe Joyce was right. Not that I'd go out with anyone else, but I'd just ignore the Marcie Gerard bit. He didn't show. I waited for him at lunch, and when I couldn't find him in the cafeteria I called his house.

Mrs. Perna answered. "Oh, yes, Beth. Didn't Kenny tell you? He went out to the college to arrange his schedule. He won't be back until Wednesday."

No, Mrs. Perna, he didn't tell me. But all I said out loud was "Oh." Usually I knew what Kenny was doing all the time. It wasn't like him to go on a trip and not let me know.

On Wednesday when he still hadn't shown, I swallowed that big blob of pride in my throat and called Mrs. Perna again. "Kenny decided to make one more stop, Beth. He won't be back until Friday."

Terrific. And not even a postcard. Dad was working late hours again, so I ate with Grandma and Aunt Nina. It seemed silly to fight Grandma about it. Besides, her cooking was a little better than TV dinners.

On Thursday Aunt Nina called me into the living room. We both looked at her legs. It was still very fine, but there was definitely hair covering her from ankles to thigh.

"When do you think you'll be able to film, Aunt Nina?"

"Oh, I think another couple of days." She ran her hands over her legs. "Listen, Beth honey, I've a favor to ask of you."

Uh oh. Aunt Nina had her buy-my-shampoo-and-you'll-be-as-gorgeous-as-me voice on. I knew something must be coming.

"Beth, Grandma has to go to the doctor tomorrow. Just a check on her blood pressure. Do you think you could go with her?" She ran her hands over her legs again.

Her legs were no excuse for not going out. "Aunt Nina, if you wear pants, no one is going to be able to tell whether you have hairy legs or not."

"I know, Beth." Her voice was what Daddy called Lauren Bacall sultry. "It's just that I absolutely hate doctors and medicines and pills. And Grandma actually enjoys her examinations. They're the highlight of her week. She can absolutely embarrass you to death in the office. Janet . . ." Aunt Nina rustled the magazine in her lap. "Your mother always took her. You know how Grandma and I fight. We get along like sand caught in the seat of a bathing suit. If I go with her, it'll take a month for us all to recover."

You just couldn't be mad at Aunt Nina. Not only was she gorgeous and funny but she was honest too. Part of her charm, Mother used to say.

"I absolutely can't handle her in doctors' offices. She'll be good with you."

It was true. Mother always took Grandma to the doctor. Of course, I'm sure Aunt Nina didn't know that Mom'd slam things around the house for two days after. Still it was hard to refuse Aunt Nin.

She continued. "I made the appointment. Right after school. You can meet her at the office." Mother always drove, of course. "I'll call a cab and you call one when you're ready to come home."

I agreed. Joyce was supposed to come over tomorrow, to give me moral support while I tried to call Kenny again, but what else could I do?

It wasn't Friday the thirteenth but it might have been. Everything went wrong. Marcie Gerard went out of her way to give me a big smile and a "Hi!" All week I had been noticing how tiny her nose was. Joyce told me she had had a nose job two summers ago, and it was certainly gorgeous. I fingered my own bump. Well, I still had longer eyelashes.

Then Joyce and I were kept after class by our history teacher who wanted to check footnotes on our Wars of the Roses report. I kept glancing at the clock, until he said, "I hope I'm not boring you, Ms. Frankle. However, this is one-third of your history mark for the term."

Quickly I explained about my grandmother's appointment, and after keeping us a little longer (just to prove he wasn't going to give in easily), he let us leave.

Grandma had been waiting in the office maybe five minutes, but from the way she carried on with the nurses, you would have thought it was three days. I was embarrassed to claim her.

Finally her name was called. "Come, Beth, you go in with me."

"Gram, I'll be waiting right out here."

Grandma looked as if she were going to cry. "Janet always went in with me. What if Dr. Steiner wants to tell a member of the family something special?"

There was a pay phone in the hall and I wanted to call Kenny while Gram was inside, but I was stuck again. I sighed and walked her into the examining room.

Twenty exhausting minutes later we were finished. I don't know how Dr. Steiner could ever tell the family anything special about Grandma because she knew everything about herself. Grandma knew her medical chart backwards and forwards. She had practically memorized her blood pressure for the past five years and reminded Dr. Steiner that he hadn't weighed her in two visits.

I kept wondering if Mrs. Perna would remember to tell Kenny that I had called him all week.

We were finally on our way. "Now, Beth," Grandma said, "you heard him. I've got to cut down on salty foods."

Dr. Steiner had said, "Everything's fine, Mrs. Bernstein. Keep up the good work."

"Maybe you can walk around the corner and pick me up some salt-free rolls."

"But, Grandma, the cab is here and Joyce is supposed to come over this afternoon."

"Never mind then. We'll take the cab. I'll go tomorrow after services. So, I won't have bread tonight."

I was beginning to understand why Mother had thrown things when she returned from one of these trips.

"Wait here, Grandma. It'll just take me a minute." Salt-free rolls, when all I wanted to do was talk to Kenny. A picture of Aunt Nina stretched out on the couch growing her hair flashed through my mind as I ran to the bakery.

By the time we got home, it was too late for Joyce to come over. Aunt Nina was still on the couch. I wondered if Kenny was home yet. As Grandma recited her medical bulletin, I tried to sneak out the door.

"Beth," Grandma must have a third eye tucked in the back of her bun, "go hang your coat up and come right down. We'll eat."

"No!"

Aunt Nina looked over the book she was reading. "Something wrong, Beth?"

"No, Aunt Nin. I think I'll just throw in a TV dinner. I've got lots of homework."

Grandma was choking on the words "TV dinner," but she did manage to gulp out, "But it's Friday, Shabbes, we have to

eat dinner together." I slammed the door before I had to listen
to the rest.

It was lucky I decided to go upstairs. Kenny called. I didn't
even have time to unbutton my coat.

"Beth?"

"Hi, Ken." I had thought about it all week. I wasn't going
to bring up her name. I had blocked it from my mind.

"Can you get out for a while?"

"Sure. My father isn't coming home 'til late."

"I'll be right over."

"Just honk, I'll come right down."

"OK."

"Kenny?"

"Yes?"

"Unless you'd rather pick up Marcie Gerard?" He hung
up. Now what had made me say that? Cool. I had promised
myself to be cool. I just had time to brush my teeth and pat
some musk oil through my hair. And on my temples and
throat. The pulses. That's what Aunt Nina said. You had to
cover the pulses.

It was almost like normal time. He drove around the cul-
de-sac, where the street dead-ended, and parked.

I didn't realize how much you could miss kissing. For a
couple of minutes while we were wrapped around each other,
I didn't think at all. Just felt. My heart was pounding and a
delicious tingle started at my scalp and traveled up and down
my body.

"Let's talk." Kenny was coming up for air. I realized that
the steering wheel was pressing into my side. But it didn't matter.

I pulled his head back down. "Not yet." It flashed through my mind that I was acting a little hungrier for kisses than he was.

He carefully untangled a strand of my hair that had caught on his jacket button. "Nice to have you back."

"Hmmm. Nice to be back." I had to reach for his head again.

"Beth." He pushed my hand away. "C'mon, you know the back of my neck is ticklish."

"Yes, I know! Does Marcie Gerard?" I traced the bumps behind his ears and bent my head so he couldn't see my red face. Why couldn't I learn to keep my mouth shut?

"OK. I know you heard about Marcie. That's what I love about this school. Everybody puts you in a closed box. You do one thing different, like being seen with another girl, and everyone's on you. That's why I can't wait to get away to college."

I couldn't figure out exactly what he meant, but I didn't like it. My hands felt cold. Is that what going with me was, being in a box? When he was in college, would he just laugh when he thought about the good kid he went around with in high school?

"Hey, come on." He grabbed my hands and pulled me close. "I'm tired of you walking around with such a sad face. We've got two-and-a-half months before I leave and I want it to be a blast."

"Marcie Gerard?" I asked.

Before he put his lips on mine, he said, "Who's she?" I didn't answer. And for the next twenty minutes, no one bothered to talk at all.

Eleven

During the next two weeks, Kenny and I seemed to be closer than ever. We saw each other every day and called each other in between times. We hit every party, game, and gathering there was. I knew I wouldn't be invited to all these things if it hadn't been for Kenny. Everyone liked him. To tell the truth, I could have skipped some of it for a little more time alone together. One Saturday night Dad had a dinner date with a couple that he and Mother had been friendly with. So I didn't feel as if I were leaving him alone when I went with Kenny. The following weekend, he got tickets to the Knicks game and took Kenny and me.

It was awkward when we got home. Daddy had driven to New York. Kenny's car was parked in front of our house.

"Well, kids, I'll see you. Unless you want to come up for a while, Kenny? Or maybe you and Beth would like to go to the diner for a snack."

Kenny looked at me. I knew Daddy was trying to be diplomatic. We all had had fun at the game, laughing and cheering for the Knicks. I had eaten myself silly; a hot dog, popcorn, even cotton candy, so I certainly wasn't hungry. But this was the special time alone that belonged to Kenny and me. Daddy put the key in the door.

"See you, Kenny. You have your key, don't you, Beth?"

His voice was bright, but his shoulders drooped. He must be losing weight. I realized that the back of his jacket was hanging in loose folds, and it took him two turns to open the door.

"You know, Ken, I'm pretty tired myself. I'll talk to you tomorrow, OK?" Even though my father's back was to us, I kissed Kenny quickly and pulled away before he had a chance to kiss me back.

"Wait up, Dad. I'll go with you."

Kenny put his hands in his pockets. I watched his body stiffen. Please, I said to myself. Please, Kenny, understand. Listen to how slowly my father is walking up the stairs. It's just been six weeks.

But Kenny walked away. I would have felt better if he had slammed the car door, but I hardly heard it click.

Monday morning I had a cold. Or maybe I was just feeling tired because Kenny hadn't called since Saturday. I tried him on Sunday, but hung up when I heard his voice. Which was silly. But I couldn't help wondering if he thought he was in a box again—when it really seemed to me that I was the one in the box, since he blew whenever I did something out of the ordinary.

Gram brought me the mail. She knew I was home from school and wanted to rub my chest with Vicks and have me hold my head over a steaming kettle to open my sinuses. She settled for watching me sip hot tea with lemon and honey.

Before she went back down, she tapped one of the envelopes.

"I told you it would start."

"What do you mean, Gram?"

"Smell!"

She held out a cream-colored envelope with "Mr. Steven Frankle" written in violet ink with lacy loops and swirls. Even with my clogged nose, the smell of lilacs wafted off the paper. As a matter of fact, the whole pile of mail smelled from that perfume, including the thick department store catalog.

Grandma was watching, but I flipped it aside. She was practically vibrating but didn't have enough nerve to ask me to open it. I made up my mind that I was going to stop being influenced by other people's fears. She finally left.

I went into my room and turned on the TV. A grinning overweight housewife who looked as if she had springs in her shoes kept jumping up and down, hugging and kissing the announcer every time she answered a question correctly.

I watched her win a refrigerator and a clock-radio, lose a set of matched luggage, and finally, just as she was going for the grand prize—a trip to Las Vegas for two—I walked back into the living room and opened the envelope.

There were more lilacs when I opened the letter, as if Mrs. Benson had sealed herself inside to arrive at our home.

Hi Steve:

Just a quick note. Been thinking about you. I've seen Beth around the neighborhood and she looks well. Wondered if you've thought about attending those meetings we spoke about. Sometimes it helps to talk to other people. If a group is too much, I'd be happy to share a cup of coffee and "rap," as the kids say. Remember, I've been there too.

Sincerely,
Anita Benson

I just couldn't stop myself and afterwards I felt ashamed. But I ripped it up. I watched the purple ink disappear as I flushed away the pieces. Dad would probably laugh at the note. Grandma and Aunt Nina were making me hyper. If only she hadn't written in that purple ink and drenched the paper in perfume.

The phone rang.

"Why aren't you in school?"

My sinuses cleared, the jagged pieces in my head fell back in place, and I could swallow. Kenny!

"I have a cold."

"How did you get it?"

"Germs. Didn't you ever take biology?"

"Yeah, well, you didn't get them from me. I haven't been near you all weekend."

I didn't answer. OK, Kenny. If it makes you feel better.

He continued. "I'll stop by on the way home."

"Thanks."

"You want me to bring anything?"

"I guess some ice cream, if you want."

"See you later."

I ran the shower. I'd just have time to wash my hair and blow it dry before he got here. I hoped Gram didn't hear the water running. You weren't allowed showers when you had colds or your period. And I was not in the mood to go round the mulberry bush with her today.

The phone rang again as I came out of the shower. It was Aunt Nina. She had gone back to New York. The funny thing was, after she'd spent two-and-a-half weeks growing the hair on her legs, they had canceled the commercial. So she had to have it all waxed off again. I asked her why she didn't use the hair remover she was supposed to advertise, and she said, "Are you crazy?"

But, she explained, the company had paid her for the two weeks off and she had had a nice rest.

"Guess what, Beth? I've got an appointment this afternoon to redo that hair spray ad. Remember?"

Who could forget? Aunt Nina had been photographed with her hair flying and the wind machine had torn the sleeve right off her silk blouse and practically blown her across the room. That first session had sent her home for two days to recuperate.

She was talking about Thanksgiving. "So, sweetie, Thanksgiving is next weekend and you know how Grandma is about holidays." I sure did. On Thanksgiving she always invited some distant cousins from Brooklyn who she said didn't have a decent meal from one Thanksgiving 'til the next. And she was probably right.

"David asked me to go to San Juan with him and I could use the rest. But you and your father are planning to eat with Grandma, aren't you?"

"I guess so, Aunt Nin. I mean we always eat Thanksgiving dinner together."

"That's what I was hoping. I'm going to run in tomorrow

and grab some things and run right back to New York. Oh, by the way, how do you feel? Grandma told me you were home with a cold."

She didn't wait for my answer. "If I don't see you, have a terrific Thanksgiving and thanks for, well, you know, keeping an eye out for your grandma. And don't let her overdo in the cooking department. You know how she is when she starts her kitchen orgies. I'll bring you something gorgeous from P.R. Love ya!"

"Hey, Aunt Nin." She hung up. I rubbed my hair with the towel. I shivered as some water dripped down my neck. I was a little confused. Had I promised to help Grandma cook Thanksgiving dinner? Mother always did. The kitchen would be in a frenzy for a week before and after. Come to think of it, Aunt Nina had gone away last Thanksgiving. Or was that Passover? I couldn't remember. She always disappeared over holidays.

Dad had wanted Mother to go up to the mountains last Thanksgiving so she wouldn't knock herself out cooking. But she had said, "No, Steve, I can't leave Mom on the holidays."

"What about Nina?" he had asked.

Mother had laughed and patted him on the cheek. "She's as reliable as a butterfly. You never know if she'll stay put. If you reach out toward her, she'll fly away."

Big deal! So I would help Grandma over Thanksgiving. Kenny! I reached for the blower. Uh oh! The Thanksgiving football game. Everybody went. Football in the morning and turkey in the afternoon. Last year Kenny had given me a yellow chrysanthemum. I would help Gram the night before, set the table . . .

Night before! Pep rally. Mother and Dad had gone last

year. There was a giant bonfire and singing. Well, I would set the table in the afternoon, and Kenny and I would take Daddy to the pep rally. And next year I could get a job as a juggler in the circus. But it was settled. I wasn't a butterfly, I could handle it. The blower was hot and it stopped my shivering.

Twelve

Nothing worked out as I had planned. We might as well have crossed Thanksgiving off the calendar this year. Dad came home early Monday night. He had had a haircut and was carrying a box. "Some new shirts." He flipped the box into the air and tossed it on the couch. He smelled different too. I think he had changed his after-shave lotion. He reached into his pocket and handed me some money. "Tomorrow I want you to stop after school and buy yourself something new. We're going to Miami for the weekend."

"Miami?"

"Yes. There's some business I've got to do, so I decided to combine the trip. We'll fly down Wednesday night, take in some sun and fun, and Friday I'll take care of my appointments."

Nobody ever consulted me about anything in this life. I reviewed the whole weekend in my mind. Kenny. He had skipped basketball practice to bring me the ice cream and we had spent the rest of the afternoon making up and deciding what we'd do Thanksgiving weekend.

"What about Grandma?" I asked.

"What about her?" Dad was going through the mail. I wondered if the lilac smell was gone.

"Won't she be upset about us not spending Thanksgiving together?"

"Don't worry, your grandmother's tougher than you think. Nina will be here, and then she always invites those Brooklyn cousins for dinner."

"But Dad, Aunt Nin is going to Puerto Rico for the weekend! Grandma will be lonely without any of us here."

He threw the opened mail across the counter. "Look, Beth, you don't have to go if you don't want to." He walked over to the large easy chair and sat down. "I know you like the beach and I thought we could have some time alone to catch up with each other. But it's okay. I'll go myself. I've got to get away for a while."

He closed his eyes and suddenly my stomach dropped. Even with the fresh shave his face was gray looking, or maybe it was the dark shadows underneath his eyes. I didn't like the new after-shave smell. The barber must have talked him into it. My father needed some sun and he needed me.

"Of course I want to go, Daddy. It's just that I promised to help Grandma with the cooking and stuff."

"You've done more than your share of helping. You're too young to be stuck in a kitchen the whole weekend. Get yourself a sexy bikini. I want to watch all the lifeguards in Miami flip their whistles." He stood up and paced. "But either way, sweetheart, I'm going. I've got to change the scenery for a few days. I just can't sit through a holiday meal and listen to your grandmother carry on about Janet—your mother."

I knew what he meant. Sometimes I think Grandma feels that if she doesn't cry at least once a day, we'll all forget Mother. Still, I could get away by going to the football game and spending Thanksgiving with Kenny. It's funny, Daddy never even asks about Kenny. It's as if he thinks that stopped too when Mother died. And in a way I guess it almost did.

"I'll go, but on one condition. You tell Grandma."

He opened his eyes and laughed. "OK, chicken. You're like your mother. I'll do the dirty work. After all, I'm just a relative by marriage."

I don't know what he finally told her, but it must have been good. Grandma never said a word to me. She just walked around with her jaw a little tighter and told me to make sure I had enough clean underwear to take to Florida. But then, to Grandma, clean underwear was another remedy that righted every wrong.

"Just stay close to your father, Beth," she said. "This is a hard time for a man. I can never get another daughter and you've lost your mother, but a man can always get another wife."

She didn't know any more about my parents' marriage than anybody else if she thought Dad could just go out and get "another wife."

She also mentioned that Aunt Nina had decided to come home for Thanksgiving. Aunt Nin never called to talk to me and I felt guilty, as if I had ruined her plans for Puerto Rico.

Daddy did something really special to help Grandma with the cooking. He ordered a turkey and all the trimmings from a catering firm that specialized in kosher food. They would deliver it ready to eat Thanksgiving morning. At first Grandma hit the ceiling. Everything in her house that was served had to be made by her own hands. She didn't believe in shortcuts. Daddy was nice but firm. "Well, Mom," he said, "it's already ordered and can't be canceled. You folks will have to eat it or throw it out."

Faced with that ultimatum, she gave in. "I'm not going to throw out good money after bad." It's funny how much older Grandma seemed when she stopped fighting. Her hair was practically all white with thinning patches on the top. When she gave in, her skin sort of crumpled together. "But tell them, no noodle kugel. That I won't allow. Noodle kugel I make myself. The cousins don't come all the way from Brooklyn for store-bought kugel."

"OK, Mom, we'll hold the kugel." He reached down and gave her a hug. "But you freeze a piece for Beth and me and we'll have it as soon as we get back."

"Hmm," she sniffed, but I noticed she didn't try to push him away. "If there's any left I'll save some. But no promises. And only five minutes on each side, the two of you, when you lay in the sun. Remember, Beth, sunscreen on that nose. You know how it burns." It was all right, she was her old bossy self again.

I called Joyce and she just said, "Oh, Beth, Thanksgiving."

"I know, but I can't let my father go alone."

"No, you can't do that. Just think, you'll come back all tanned and gorgeous and we'll be all white-faced and blah."

"Yeah, if it doesn't rain."

"Let me know what Kenny says when you tell him."

Kenny! There I was again. I met him Tuesday in the cafeteria at lunch. I had the split lunch period but decided to cut the first half of English so I could spend more time with him. We took our sandwiches out to his car. I ran all the way.

"Hurry, unlock the door, I'm freezing." I hadn't bothered with my coat and there was no more nice New Jersey sun. The day was overcast. It looked like snow.

I put the drink cartons on the floor between us and spread a napkin on my lap. My teeth were chattering.

"Hold on, Beth, you're cold. I'll turn on the engine for a minute and warm the car up." He flipped the ignition.

"Hey, don't do that, Ken, we'll get asphyxiated."

"I've got the window open. Here." He handed me an old sweatshirt from the backseat. I slipped it over my head. He rubbed my arms up and down quickly, the way you would rub down a swimmer who had just finished a race. "That better?" he asked.

"Hmm. Yeah!"

"Thin blood—that's what's the matter with you, girl. You've got no blood."

"I guess I was made for warmer climates. And Kenny, speaking of warmer climates . . ." I really didn't want to say it like a big joke and make believe I didn't care. Actually I like the cold. It would probably be great for the game. We would have taken blankets to sit on and wrap around our legs. Last year Mother had made us a thermos full of hot tea and I had taken a bag of donuts. Everyone around had shared sips with us and said, "Now why didn't I do that?" But that was my mother—other people thought of things, but she did them. Tommy had brought beer, but no one wanted it on such a cold day.

Kenny took a big bite of sandwich. His mother always

made him enormous bologna sandwiches with lettuce and cheeses and other kinds of spreads.

My cafeteria chicken salad tasted like cardboard, or maybe that was the dryness in my throat. I took a sip from the orange juice carton. It helped a little. When I was small, I had had a Raggedy Ann lunch box with a matching thermos. All through the lower grades, Raggedy Ann had shared lunch with me. Mother always hid something special in it, an iced cupcake or a brownie or a big star-shaped sugar cookie with colored sprinkles. The school cafeteria didn't cater to individual human tastes. As a matter of fact sometimes I wondered if they catered to human stomachs.

"Hey, you haven't said a word." Kenny had finished his sandwich and was on his milk. "I might as well be sitting here by myself." There was no way this chicken salad was going to go down.

"Listen, Ken, about Thanksgiving."

"Another problem?"

"No." I wasn't going to let him make it a problem. "My father has business in Florida and we're going to go down Wednesday night for the whole weekend."

He slurped the bottom of his milk. Kenny never slurps. "The whole weekend?"

"I'm afraid so."

"No Thanksgiving game, no pep rally, and what about our plans for Friday and Saturday night?"

"I'll be back Sunday, Ken—but late, I think."

Our breaths were steaming up the windows. Maybe it would snow. A good hard snow and then there would be no Thanksgiving game and no planes leaving for Miami and I could spend the whole weekend under the covers and wake up Monday morning with everything back in place.

He took my hand and traced the curve of my knuckles with his finger. "It's my last Thanksgiving at Millburn."

"I know, Ken."

"In February I'll be off to Penn. You know, if I want med school I'm going to have to start grinding away the minute I get there. That's why I'm not really upset about not getting a basketball scholarship. I don't think I'd be able to study and play."

It had taken him almost a year to admit that to me.

"Oh, come on, Ken, you can do it all."

"Uh, uh." He shook his head. "My old man is really serious about this. He's been on my back about med school for as long as I can remember. If I don't get the marks, he's not shelling out for school."

I didn't know what to say. Mom and Dad had never been paranoid about my marks, but then I really hadn't made up my mind what I would study in college.

"So I wanted to let loose this Thanksgiving, have a wild time."

Well, I would have loved to let loose too, but I was starting to learn that just wanting something doesn't make it happen.

"Listen, I'm not going to hassle you about Florida. But, like, it seems to me if your old man's going on business, I don't know what he needs you for."

I didn't answer. What could I say? Ken kept talking about his last Thanksgiving at Millburn. You'd think he was never going to set foot in the place again.

"So listen, babe, you do what you have to, and I'll do what I have to."

"What does that mean?"

"You don't think I'm going to stay home and watch the mail for your postcard?" The trouble is I hadn't thought about what he was going to do.

"I'm going to get a date and go to the game and out Friday and Saturday night. All the things I planned. I'd rather do them with you, but if I have to get somebody else I will."

It was logical and he was right. I shouldn't have any complaints. So why did I feel like I had a giant black-and-blue spot inside my rib cage? It wasn't just the weekend. Was it because Kenny found it so easy to tell me he could find someone else to do things with? Grandma had said it: men can always find someone else. When I thought of the game or the rally, it was always to share with Kenny. I guess I could go with someone else too, but it wouldn't be the same.

"So you go to Florida. But, Beth, you really ought to think about it. How's your father ever going to meet someone new if you're always hanging around him?"

This time it was Kenny telling me about my father's future. I picked up my sandwich again. Anything to keep my mouth busy so I wouldn't answer that one. Did Kenny think my father was like him? Just needed a girl, any girl to do things with? Well, maybe I was replaceable, but Mother wasn't.

"I don't want to hold you back, Ken. You do whatever you want. And when I come home, there'll be Christmas vacation coming up and New Year's. I don't know what my plans will be. I wouldn't want to hang you up, so why don't you just make all your plans so you won't miss out on your last Christmas at Millburn."

"If that's the way you want it, Beth."

If that's the way I wanted it! Maybe I didn't know him, but he should certainly know me better than that. I never did know how to be a good fighter. I traced my initials on the foggy window. Mother! I was angry at her. Why did she have to die? Why couldn't it be last year when everything was going so smoothly? When my biggest worry was whether I'd find the right dress to wear to the Christmas Snowball.

I walked slowly back into the building. Kenny stayed in the car. I had forgotten to take the rest of my lunch out of the car. Good, I hoped Kenny would forget too. Then it would decay and stink up the whole inside for whichever girl he replaced me with. I ached all over. I would skip the rest of the day, go to the nurse and tell her I had bad cramps and had to go home.

I thought of something Miss Brock said to me the other day. She had stopped me after class. "How's everything going for you, Beth?"

"Oh, pretty good, thanks."

"Well, you've really had a terrible blow this year, but I've been watching you handle it. These are the things that shape our futures and build our characters."

She should see my overdeveloped, musclebound character now. I think its weight is starting to knock me over.

Thirteen

The weather was glorious in Florida. Thursday morning we spent baking on the beach. I smeared myself with lots of suntan goo. The sun was gentle at first and then the rays bounced in front of my closed eyes, causing white spots in the blackness. The heat pushed my shoulders into the sand and my whole body felt limp. Finally I pushed myself up and plunged into the cold water to revive. The goose bumps reminded me of the Thanksgiving game and Kenny. I hoped he was sitting on the cold seats without a blanket and drinking ice-cold beer with Tom so that he'd be even colder. He probably had forgotten gloves too. He thought it wasn't macho to wear them even if it was twenty degrees out. I looked over at Daddy. He was stretched out on his back, eyes closed. The lines across his forehead were relaxed. I went back to my blanket to repeat the sequence of heat, wet coolness, and heat again.

We had hot dogs for lunch and then changed and headed

for the tennis courts. They were all taken and we had to put our names on a list. The pro came up to Daddy. He pointed to an end court where three men were rallying. "Mr. Frankle, there's an opening on Court Two for one player. Would you like to join them? I know the others; it's a good doubles game."

"Thanks anyway, but I don't want to leave Beth alone. We'll wait until there's an open court."

The three men were really slamming the ball to each other, hard and fast. "Oh, don't be silly, Daddy. Go play, they can give you a good workout. We'll play later."

The pro turned to me. He was cute. Very blond and very tanned. His teeth gleamed as brightly as his tennis whites. "I have some free time now. If you'd like a lesson or want to hit awhile, I have the back court."

"Good idea. I'll play if you take a lesson, Beth." Daddy was already on his feet. "Get her in shape for me." He ran on to the court and shook hands all around. The men warmed him up. He missed a couple of easy baseline shots, then he started moving quickly and getting his racket back. Daddy was a good athlete. He played most games well. He was laughing and joking as if he had known the other players all his life. He couldn't have a game like that with me.

The pro's name was Don, Don Hendricks. We decided to work on my backhand. He asked me if I were staying long. "Just for the weekend."

"Where you from?"

"New Jersey."

"You at the hotel?" He glanced up at the glass tower behind us.

"Yes."

"Like to disco? I'm on tonight, the courts are open late, but I'm free tomorrow."

"Well, I'm here with my father. I don't know what he has planned for us." He raised his eyebrows and shrugged. Joyce would have thought I was a real jerk. It was hard to make conversation. I guess I was just too used to Kenny.

The ball started to come faster as he moved me from one end of the court to the other. We didn't speak for the rest of the lesson.

Daddy was still playing when I finished, so I joined three kids who were hitting on an opposite court. They were younger than me but were good players. It was better than sitting around, and my lesson had warmed me up.

Before I realized it, we had finished two sets. "I've had it." I tossed the balls back across the court. One of the girls was about fourteen. Her name was Liz and she followed me. "Gee, you're really a good player. I like your tennis skirt. Are you here with your parents? They have a teen lounge in the hotel, do you want to go with me tonight? Otherwise my parents drag me around to the hotel shows." She talked the way she played tennis, with slap shots.

Daddy was having drinks on the sidelines with his foursome. They had been joined by their wives, and it turned out that Liz was one couple's daughter.

"The backhand looks good, Beth," Daddy called out. "How about a cold drink?" I pulled up a chair and nodded yes. There were introductions all around. Liz pulled up a chair next to me. "What do you say, Beth? Ask your father?" I was trying to think of a polite way to cut her off.

Then one of the ladies asked, "Is your wife with you, Steve? Maybe you'd like to join us for dinner."

Dad stirred one of his ice cubes with the top of his finger. He didn't look up. "My wife passed away a couple of months ago. Beth and I are just here for a few days of sunshine."

You could hear the balls slap back and forth from the courts where people were still playing. Liz sat back in her seat. Finally another woman spoke up. "The invitation still goes. Maybe you and Beth would like to join us."

"Sure," said one of the men.

The conversation picked up with the couples discussing the merits of the steaks at the different restaurants they had already visited.

I held my breath. I hadn't given up Thanksgiving at home to come to Florida and go out to eat with a bunch of strangers.

"Thanks a lot," Dad answered. "But we're just going to catch a light bite tonight. I've got business tomorrow and I want to look over some papers."

He stood up and reached for his racket. One of the ladies caught Dad's arm. "Listen, we just met and you'll probably thing this is really nervy of me."

"Nancy," her husband warned.

"But we happen to have this great friend. She lost her husband last year. Really a terrific gal. After all, Long Island isn't so far from New Jersey. Maybe when we get back home I could have everyone over, so you could meet."

"Thanks anyway." Daddy shook hands with the men. As we walked away, their voices got louder. "What's the matter with you, Nancy? We don't even know him. We only played *tennis*."

"Never mind," Nancy answered. "What's the harm? He's a great-looking guy."

"Sorry about that, Beth." Daddy gave me a hug.

"Can you help it if you're so great looking? It seems like every single lady from Great Neck to Asbury Park is going to be chasing you." I could joke now that I knew he had no intentions of getting "fixed up."

"Come on. Cut that out." But he was laughing. "Now you sound like your Aunt Nina."

I danced in front of him, bouncing a tennis ball. He bounced it back over my head and it landed in the pool. "Come on, I'm hot." He threw off his shirt and sneakers and dove in with his tennis shorts. He came up sputtering, with the tennis ball. But he looked young and happy. I was glad we had come.

We had huge corned beef sandwiches, sour pickles, and French fries for dinner. The taste of delicatessen food and my sunburned shoulders plus the palm-lined Florida landscape made me forget it was Thanksgiving. That is, until I saw a forlorn picture of two slightly crumpled Pilgrims and some tattered Indians hanging on the bulletin board of the hotel lobby. And I wondered if the girl Kenny took to the game had gotten a yellow chrysanthemum—but that made my ribs ache inside, so I wondered if Grandma had really served the store-bought turkey. And then I couldn't finish eating because I noticed that Daddy was pushing the food around on his plate and I wondered if Mother had ever shown any early symptoms of her hemorrhage that we all had been too busy to notice.

Dad left early in the morning. I took another tennis lesson from Don. "The invitation still holds for tonight," he said.

"Thanks, but do you think we could work on my serve for a while?"

"It's your lesson, you're the boss." And he whacked the ball so hard at me that it bounced off the wood of my racket.

I kept my nose buried in a book the rest of the afternoon. I saw Liz around the swimming pool and I was sure she was trying to track me down. I thought of calling Joyce to find out who Kenny had taken to the game, but I decided to save the money. I'd get the bad news for free on Monday.

I must have drifted off in the heat when I heard Dad's voice. "Hey, sun goddess, wake up."

He grabbed my toes. I opened my eyes, then shut them quickly against the glare of the sun. "Come on, Beth, I want you to meet someone."

I adjusted my sunglasses. The dancing white spots disappeared. In their place stood Daddy dressed in slacks and a sport shirt open at the collar. There was color in his face and his eyes were brighter. And next to him was a tall blond woman, a female version of the tennis pro. Tanned, white teeth, and lots of tumbling yellow hair on her shoulders. Did they grow these people on orange trees down here?

"Beth, this is Stacy Arnold. She's Marty's associate. I invited her to have a drink with us."

For a minute I figured the sun had melted parts of my brain. Marty was the guy Daddy was here to see on business. Stacy Arnold had on skintight jeans and a white polo shirt. She looked like a movie star.

"How are you, Beth?" She held out her hand. "No one would believe you had such a *big* daughter, Steve." The way she put the accent on "big" I got the feeling she was staring at my nose.

Dad spoke up. "Let's have a cold drink." They waited while I grabbed my beach robe and we went into the bar. The air conditioning was cold against my hot skin, though I was glad for the suntan because I was sure my cheeks must be flaming red. Daddy had one arm around me and the other very casually around Stacy Arnold.

They ordered Bloody Marys. I had a Coke.

"So, Beth Frankle. What do you do when you're not lying around a Florida pool?" Stacy Arnold was going to be cutesy-poo to me.

"I'm a junior in high school." But apparently Stacy Arnold wasn't going to be cutesy-poo or try to win me over. As a matter of fact, she didn't even wait for my answer before she started talking to Dad.

"Well, how about it, Steve? It's open house at Marty's tonight. Why don't you and . . ." She had to turn back to me again, "and Beth join us all? Some drinks, a couple of laughs."

One of Grandma's health rules: don't drink ice-cold soda when you've been out in the hot sun. She must be right. The two temperatures were mixing somewhere in the middle of my stomach while I waited for Daddy to tell this Stacy that we were going to the movies. He didn't.

"Sounds like fun." He sipped his drink. He and Stacy were looking at each other. "How about it, Beth? Shall we try a Florida open house?"

Was Grandma right? Or was all this sudden attention going to his head? Wasn't I company enough for him? Oh, I could understand about the tennis game. I was the one who had even told him to play with people who were equal to him. But women wanting to fix him up, lilac letters—no, that wasn't fair, he had never even seen that letter. But we had come to Florida, or rather I had come, to spend time together. He had been so sad at home. The hanging jacket, the gray look. I had given up my plans in a minute. I thought we'd have a chance to open up to each other. I wanted to tell him how much I missed Mother and I wanted to hear the same from him.

"Beth?" He was waiting for me to answer and there was a little-boy look on his face, like someone waiting to be given permission. How had I suddenly become responsible for the whole world? And this Stacy, she looked about twenty-two. She probably thinks my father is a rich old man dying to get married. Though I realize that no way could my father be considered an old man.

They were waiting for me to answer. Stacy had her arm draped across his shoulder. Like she was planting the flag of possession.

"I don't think so, Dad. Why don't you and . . . and Stacy go?"

The brightness went out of his face and the gray was back. "Is everything all right, Beth? Do you feel OK?"

"Perfect. Go ahead, Dad . . ." My eyes caught something white streak in front of the glass-enclosed bar. "Anyway, the tennis pro asked me to go dancing or something tonight . . ."

Stacy grabbed my hand. I had finally gotten her attention. "That's terrific, Beth. I'm sure you wouldn't want to be with us old folks anyway . . ." She said "old folks" with a flutter of eyelashes that meant the exact opposite. "See, Steve? Aren't you glad you came to Florida?"

Dad had brightened again. "Beth, if you're sure?"

He believed me! "I'm positive, Dad. I was just waiting to see if you were set."

He didn't hesitate. "OK, Ms. Arnold, you and I have a date."

She gave him a hug and said, "I'll pick you up in the front lobby at eight!" She shook her car keys in a good-bye wave that excluded me. Daddy stood like a little boy set loose in the train department of F. A. O. Schwarz. "Hey, Stacy, how should I dress?"

This is my father, who opens elevator doors and whisks you to the best table at crowded restaurants, asking a bouncing T-shirt what he should wear?

"*Casual!*" She blew a kiss across the cocktail lounge. He turned back to me.

"She runs Marty's office single-handed. She's only twenty-eight, has an M.A. in business administration, and handles a staff of fifty. She's computer trained, was married once, and has her own condominium on the beach. She flies all over for Marty . . ."

I was about to ask him if she also made tasty casseroles. Some business trip, if he had so much time to find out everything about Stacy Arnold!

"I'm going up, Beth. Want to shower and relax. You coming up?"

We had adjoining rooms. "No, Dad, I think I'll catch more sun."

"OK. See you later." Didn't he notice that my nose was

beet-red already, and I would probably blister the way I always did from too much sun? But he threw some money down on the bar and hurried off. WHISTLING!

I walked back into the sun and this time the reverse happened. The hot rays made me shiver. I looked back into the cocktail lounge, but Dad was gone. He hadn't noticed the tiny bumps that were moving up and down my bare arms and legs.

I don't think I had breathed the whole time we were in the lounge. I took a breath now and the sun spots were back in front of my eyes. I walked quickly over to the tennis courts.

Don was in the pro shop leaning against a stack of sweaters. He must have given a dozen lessons but still looked immaculate in those tennis whites.

"Well, look who's here. Miss Beth Frankle."

"Yeah. Well, there's been a change of plans and I was wondering if you still, well . . ." I tried to think how Joyce would say it, but I was stumbling.

"You mean you can make it tonight?"

"I think so. I mean, yes I can."

"Good—8:30, front lobby."

"Fine, uh . . ." I turned to go. "Oh, by the way, Don, how should I dress?"

Funny how a word can rip right through you. "Casual," was his answer.

Fourteen

Daddy was dressed before I was, but then he had an ear-
lier date. "Date." I didn't like that word at all. The door
was open between our rooms. He knocked once before
walking in.

"Aren't you dressed yet, Beth?"

"I took my shower already, but I'm not going out until
8:30."

"How do I look?" he asked. Again he acted unsure about
himself. He sucked in his stomach and looked in the mirror. I
could smell the Aramis. The new after-shave hadn't lasted too
long. He had on an open silk shirt. A gold-link chain was fas-
tened tightly around his neck. My mother had given it to him
for winning a golf tournament last summer. He also wore a
longer gold chain with a twenty-dollar gold piece attached.
Mother had given him the gold piece for his fortieth birthday,
and Gram, Aunt Nina, and I had bought the chain.

He sat down on the edge of the bed and took a breath.

"Maybe I should call Stacy. I think I'm a little too old for this." His shoulders slumped. I hadn't wanted him to go, but I didn't want him like this, so lonely looking and unsure of himself.

"Oh, come on, Dad. Get up, you'll probably meet a lot of interesting people."

"Yeah, but Stacy may be a little too much for me. After all, I'm a little out of practice for this singles scene. Standing around making conversation with strangers."

"Then Stacy Arnold's probably the perfect one to be with. From what you say about her, all you have to do is stay on your feet. She'll take care of the rest."

He laughed. "Yeah, I guess you're right. Well, I've got to make my debut sometime." Why, I wanted to ask. But he was smiling and up on his feet. "I guess I'll go downstairs. You'll probably be back late, so I'll see you in the morning." He hesitated, twisting the door knob. "Have a good time, hon." *I* would probably be back late! It was amazing how everything got dumped on me.

I started to dress. Casual. Let's see. Jeans or slacks? Slacks or jeans? How come there was no one around to give *me* confidence? What the heck did "casual" mean down here? Kenny and I always went around in jeans. We had matching turtleneck sweaters that we had bought at the start of football season. I settled on black linen slacks with a striped sweater. After I had my hair all brushed, I decided the outfit was too dressy. So I changed to jeans. My good jeans and a white polo that had gobs of color dripping from a sign that said "WET PAINT!" I searched through the drawer again. There was a solid red polo. I held it up against me. No, I would keep on the "WET PAINT!"

It was 8:15. I slipped the hotel key and some money into a macrame shoulder bag. Dad and Stacy were probably gone by now. I could go downstairs.

Once Mom and I had had a discussion about people remarrying. Grandma had told us about a man who remarried three months after his wife died. She thought it was disgusting. Mom didn't agree and said it showed that he had a good marriage if he wanted to remarry so quickly.

My throat was tight. There were so many people in the lobby. Don Hendricks was probably a great dancer. I hoped I could keep up. I'm good, but then I'm used to Kenny's style. I haven't danced with a lot of other guys.

"Here I am. All ready?" He looked even cuter at night. My throat eased a little. He was wearing jeans and a tennis shirt open at the neck. I had guessed right about the clothes.

Don took my arm and we walked out through the front. People were looking at us and he was smiling and waving.

"Hi, Don. Don't forget we have a lesson at ten tomorrow."

"Sure thing, Mrs. Warner." That woman had to be at least forty. She reminded me of Mrs. Benson the way she tugged on Don's arm. Poor Mrs. Benson, I wondered if she had a date tonight. I'll bet Stacy Arnold never went to Parents Without Partners socials. Of course she wasn't a parent. But I couldn't imagine her having trouble getting to know anyone she wanted to. When I go home, maybe I'll tell Mrs. Benson to go to Miami and take tennis lessons.

Don had a battered Volkswagen. You had to sit close, the front seat was so small. With every sway of the car, I felt his big shoulders pressing into mine. And my sunburn was stinging. I wondered what kind of car Stacy Arnold had. Probably something little, but expensive. Foreign, like a Mercedes.

Don must be used to quiet girls, or else he thought what he had to say was more interesting than anything else. In the few minutes it took to get to the disco I learned his past, present, and future. How he was number one on the tennis team in college. How this was just an interim job, to save enough to get on the pro tour. How he had won the Junior Men's Regional Championship two years ago. How every hotel in Miami was begging for his services. How the ladies tipped him. How his cross-court passing shot was equal to John Newcombe's. How he needed more practice on grass. And how next year I would be able to watch him play tennis on TV at the U.S. Open.

The music was deafening. The speakers were set at angles all over the ceiling. No matter how you turned you couldn't escape. Strobe lights flashed across the dancers and made them look as if they were moving in stilted slow motion, like characters in an old-fashioned movie. When you got closer, you could see their bodies moving in double time, whipped up by the beat. We sat on one of the low, cushioned lounges which surrounded the dance floor. The place was crowded and full of smoke. Don shouted that it wouldn't really start jumping until after eleven.

A waitress dressed in a mini and tight blouse took our order. "Hi, Donnie. What'll you have?"

He looked at me. I guess this was the kind of place that wasn't going to ask your age. I'd feel silly ordering ginger ale; he'd probably think I was a baby. All I could think of was a white wine spritzer. Mother always ordered that. She didn't like hard liquor.

Don ordered vodka and tonic. I was going to ask him if John Newcombe drank that when he was in top form but decided it wasn't worth the shout. More people came in. The waiters just plunked down small tables and everybody had to scrunch together on the lounges. I was practically sitting on Don's lap. Grandma wouldn't have to worry about me putting elbows on the table, because there was no room to even move your arms.

"Let's dance." Don reached for my hand and pulled me up to the dance floor. It was a fast hustle. He was a better dancer than Kenny. At first I had trouble with some of the turns, but he was a great leader and when I relaxed I found that I was spinning out and in without any effort. My body just couldn't ignore the drums and guitar beat. You almost didn't have to dance. The vibrations from the floor were enough to move your feet. It was a long fast set and then the bright lights were turned down and a slow ballad began to echo throughout the hall. Don pulled me close. I could feel sweat on his hair as he held me tighter and I reached up to push my own hair away from his cheek. More couples came on the floor and everybody swayed together.

A bright silver ball with hundreds of diamond shapes was hanging from the middle of the ceiling. It began to turn and a spotlight focused on it, causing thousands of spinning white spots to reflect in the dark room. I watched the white spots touch my hands and Don's face. It made you dance even closer. His body felt nice, but I missed Kenny's shoulders. My neck was twisted to the side. I couldn't get it into a comfortable position.

Maybe my father was dancing at the open house. Mother used to complain that he didn't like to dance. He was a "watcher." I didn't think Stacy Arnold would be a "watcher."

I closed my eyes against the white spots. Don breathed into my ear. "Let's move on."

We had barely touched our drinks. I sipped a little while he paid the check.

We stopped at two more discos, each one a replica of the first. Except that at one the waitresses wore Chinese dresses slit up to the hip, and at the other they were dressed like Playboy bunnies.

Don had a vodka and tonic at each place and I stuck to my white wine spritzer. I never got a chance to finish a complete drink because we danced a full set and then left for the next stop.

I couldn't believe it was twelve o'clock and we were back in the car. Don reached for me before he turned on the motor. It was a long kiss and I didn't pull away. "Baby, baby, I've been waiting all night for that." He ran his hands up and down my arm and kissed me again. I wasn't worried. After all we were in the middle of a parking lot in Miami Beach and besides, after all the music and closeness, it felt good.

He started the engine. "Where are we going now?" I asked.

"Sweetheart, I stay in one of the cabanas off the tennis courts. I've got a refrigerator there and something nice and cold to drink."

He drove quickly and sang along with the radio, reaching over every once in awhile to pat my thigh. Now I was getting nervous. A cabana wasn't a parking lot.

"Don, I really think I better go upstairs."

"Oh, come on, Beth, you're not going to turn into one of those teases, are you? I've been feeling that hot little body all night."

He parked in a spot behind the tennis courts. I followed him to the row of cabanas. I would just stay a few minutes. I didn't want him to think I was a baby. Besides, I was sure my father wasn't back yet.

He grabbed for me as soon as the door opened. Didn't even turn on the lights. This time I wasn't too happy with the kiss. My lips were closed and his tongue kept pressing against them. Finally he let go, flicked on a lamp, and opened the refrigerator. The cabana was like a one-room efficiency apartment. He took out a bottle of wine and two glasses. I shook my head.

"No thanks, Don, I really don't want any more."

"Don't be silly, baby. You didn't finish one whole drink tonight." At least someone noticed what I did. I took the wine from him. We clicked glasses in midair. "To Beth." We took a sip and clicked again.

It was my turn. "To the U.S. Open!" I was finally getting into the swing of things. He laughed, took a sip, and put his glass down. "I've got a couple of joints here. How 'bout it?"

"No thanks." There had been enough pot in the air of those discos to get high from just breathing.

He wrapped himself around me and pushed me back on the couch. Somehow he had managed to turn on the radio with one hand because soft music drifted into the room. I was still vibrating from the constant disco beat. He traced the letters on my polo—slowly. "WET PAINT!" And then again. His fingers gently trailing across my chest left tingles in their wake.

I don't know how long it would have gone on, but he reached for the zipper in front of my jeans. It was stuck. "Damn it." He had to take his lips off mine to look down at my pants. He tried to yank it, but it wouldn't move. Then he tried with both hands and that took care of the mood. What was I doing with this guy in a cabana in Miami Beach? I pushed his hands away. He didn't look so cute. As a matter of fact, there were lots of crinkles from the sun around his eyes and he smelled from the cigarettes he had been smoking all evening.

I wondered just when he had won the Junior Men's singles and somehow I didn't think he would be going to the U.S. Open this year.

I stood up. "I've got to go, Don."

"Hey, come on, you're not going to walk out now, are you?"

I measured the distance to the door. But I was silly. He wouldn't force me. Just the same I started inching my way.

"Hey, come on. You're not going to leave me like this, are you?"

"Thanks a lot, Don. But I've really got to go."

He reached for a cigarette. "Boy, how old did you say you were?"

"I didn't!"

"My mistake. I thought you were grown up."

"I'm sorry. Maybe that lady who spoke to you in the lobby is still around." I opened the door.

He made one more try. He walked over and put his arms around me. "Baby, I don't force anyone, but you got me all hot and bothered and now you're running away. I won't be able to sleep all night."

"Take a cold shower!" And I left, running behind the courts, past the darkened swimming pool, until I saw the lights from the hotel cocktail lounge. I tried to straighten my hair before I entered the bright lobby. I tucked my polo shirt back into my jeans, glancing down as if there might be fingerprints on the front of it.

The elevator took me right up. I fumbled with my key and was finally in my room. I threw myself across the bed. My heart was thumping and I couldn't catch my breath. There was a soft knock at the door. First I thought it was Don. Then the knock was louder and I realized it was coming from the door to Daddy's room.

"Beth?" It was Daddy.

I caught my breath and whispered back. "Yes?"

"Everything all right?"

"Fine."

"Did you have a good time?"

"Yeah." I waited. "Did you?"

"It was OK. I was more tired than I thought. So I left the party a little early."

I wished suddenly that I was a little girl and that my parents could tuck me in and kiss me good night. But I wasn't and I didn't have parents anymore, only a father.

"Sleep late, Beth, and we'll have breakfast by the pool."

"Good night, Daddy."

Fifteen

We flew back to New Jersey late the next day. Grandma must have been listening for us. Her door opened as we tried to go upstairs.

"Well, the travelers are back."

"Hi, Gram."

"Hi, Mom." Daddy shifted the suitcase in his hand and kissed Grandma on her forehead.

"Glad you remembered where you live."

"Did you have a nice Thanksgiving, Grandma?" I had my shoulder bag in one hand and a cosmetic case balanced in the other.

"As nice as possible, seeing my one son-in-law and my only grandchild were nowhere in sight."

Daddy started to move. "We'll talk tomorrow, Mom. Beth and I are tired. The plane was late."

"Sure. Go ahead." Grandma turned to go back inside. "You didn't use any lotion on your nose, Beth. You're all peeling and bright red. Put some Noxzema on when you go to sleep."

Before I could stop myself I touched my nose. There was a loose piece of skin. Sure enough, I was peeling and would be red and scabby looking instead of golden brown.

Joyce wasn't at the bus stop the next morning and I didn't see her until English. We hugged each other.

"You look dynamite, Beth!"

"My nose is peeling."

"You can't even see it. You look fabulous. Did you have a good time?"

I recited the story of my conquest of Don, the tennis pro. I didn't leave out any details. Joyce and I told each other everything. That wasn't exactly true. I never told her about my private moments with Kenny, but with Don Hendricks it really didn't matter.

I was going into so much detail that I didn't notice Miss Brock holding the class up waiting to get my attention. When I finally turned around, she announced:

"Well, Beth Frankle, I guess Thanksgiving vacation loosened you up. However, since the rest of us weren't lucky enough to go south for the holiday, would you mind joining us back here with some American writers?"

She should team up with Grandma; the only thing she missed was my sunburn peel.

After class I asked and Joyce told me. Kenny had been seen with Marcie Gerard for most of the Thanksgiving weekend. That's OK, I told myself. I'll see him, we'll talk, and everything will be beautiful. We can spend the whole Christmas vacation making up lost time. I started composing long letters

in my head, letters that I would write when he was away at
Penn. He would come home weekends and I would go there
to visit.

Without realizing it, I had changed my pattern of walking.
Usually we waited until lunch to meet. But I found myself
outside the boys' locker room when I knew he would be coming out.

Apparently Marcie now had a copy of his schedule because
I saw her on the other side of the water fountain. He walked
out, hair slicked down from a shower. His gym bag was under
one arm and his books under the other. He looked so good. I
don't know how I could ever have thought Don Hendricks was
cute. I moved away from the wall to call out to Kenny. I knew
everything would be great. He shifted his books, threw an arm
around Marcie, and walked off down the hall. I don't think he
even saw me.

You will not cry. You will not cry. I repeated it to myself
over and over as I watched the clock in physics class until I
couldn't stand it and asked to leave the room. I walked up and
down the hall. Maybe I should just cut and go home.

He knew I'd be back today. Why didn't he look for me?
We could make up. One weekend, and a whole year just goes
down the drain?

I waited for Joyce after school. We both watched Marcie
get in his car, toss her books on the backseat, and snuggle
close to him. Just the way I used to. As a matter of fact, it
looked like she fit right into my spot. Once Kenny had told me
that the seat was just for me, my imprint was on it. Nobody
could fit like I did. Marcie seemed to be fitting pretty good,
unless the car seat was as fickle as Kenny.

I waited for him to call or even notice that I was back. On Wednesday we collided with each other outside the cafeteria. "How are you doing, Beth? How was Florida?" He was halfway down the hall before I could even answer. Almost as if he were too embarrassed to face me.

Later in the week Joyce told me he was taking out Rhoda Alper, secretary of the senior class. Five other girls made sure to bump me and give the same information. It's nice how anxious people are to give you news like that. Rhoda Alper was a good match for him. She was one of the most popular girls in the senior class. I had always thought she had a boyfriend in college. Well, maybe she was like Kenny and wanted to leave Millburn High in a blaze of parties.

Joyce wanted to fix me up. "Come on, don't be a jerk. There are other fish in the sea, birds in the sky, roosters on the farm, giraffes in the zoo."

No matter how hard she tried, I just couldn't seem to catch the spirit. The thought of starting with someone new and having to make new conversation and learn what he liked and smile and make jokes—it just seemed like too much effort. Then after you did all that, he'd just up and leave you anyway. Or attack you like Don Hendricks.

Things were changing at home too. We cleaned out Mother's closet. I didn't want to, but Daddy insisted. "It's not healthy to leave it here as if it's a shrine to her, Beth."

I didn't think it was a shrine, but the hall closet was empty without her car coat. And the bathroom shelves looked different without her cosmetics. He gave me all her jewelry, everything except a thin gold bangle that he saved for Aunt Nina.

We were lucky Friday night. The Sisterhood was having a special Shabbes dinner and Grandma was going. For once she didn't push us to go. Dad and I went out for pizza. "How about a movie, Beth?"

"Not tonight, Dad. Joyce is coming over, remember? We're working on the yearbook project."

"You have to do it tonight?"

"We've got to get started. Joyce and the staff have been nice; they've been waiting for me. But I kind of promised I'd get to work. We do have a printing deadline."

He met some old neighbors of ours as he was paying the check.

"Dad." I was getting impatient. I'd promised Joyce I'd meet her at 7:30. She'd be standing outside freezing. "Dad." I felt like a two-year-old pulling on my father's jacket to get his attention. I couldn't wait to learn to drive. I'd be able to move around more freely by myself. Then I felt bad. After all, what did Dad have to rush home for?

Joyce was waiting. "Hi, Mr. Frankle, Beth." She was loaded down with papers. All the seniors had filled out questionnaires. Joyce and I had thought of a special "I Remember" section to be the centerfold of the yearbook. Everyone was asked to write down specific memories. They could be funny or serious, like "I remember cutting Miss Purcell's English class," or "I remember striking for more peanut butter on the sandwiches in the cafeteria." The yearbook would be published in June, but some of the seniors like Kenny and Rhoda (and other brains of the class) were leaving early to start college in February. We had to get things compiled in case we needed more information from them. It was a real coup for Joyce and me to be given this assignment as juniors. It put us in line to be editors next year for our own class yearbook.

I could have accelerated my subjects and finished early too. But Mother had been against it. "You have your whole life ahead of you," she said. "Don't rush through any part of it."

We spread the papers over my bed. Joyce sat at my desk and plugged in the typewriter. I could hear Daddy in the other room. He turned on the TV. "Will the noise bother you girls?"

"No, Mr. Frankle, I don't even hear it. At home my two brothers are always blasting their stereos, so noise doesn't affect me."

We tried to put the questionnaires in alphabetical order. I leafed through quickly, looking for Kenny's. There it was: "Kenneth Alan Perna." Then the list of his credits, which took up half a page. We weren't concerned with those. I could have recited them by heart anyway. I got to the "I remember."

Kenny Perna declared that out of three-and-a-half years of high school, he remembered "Basketball, Beck's Bunsen Burners, and my Beat-up Buick." That was it. Three Bs and no "Beth." I looked at some of the others. A fellow named Howard remembered R. S. I knew that was his girl. And lots of the girls, of course, weren't so shy. They named Jack or Michael or close dancing at the Junior Prom.

"You know, Joyce, maybe these 'I remembers' are a stupid idea."

She looked up. "Why, Beth?"

"Oh, I don't know. Maybe in twenty years when they read the yearbook all they'll remember is cutting English or Bunsen burners."

She grabbed Kenny's out of my hand and read it. "I thought so. You know that's just Kenny being clever. Look at the date." It had been filled out way before my trip to Florida, so he couldn't be using it to get back at me. I guess he was entitled to remember or be remembered as he thought fit.

I heard my father moving around in the other room. He had turned the TV off. "Hey, Beth, did the new *Time* come?"

"It's on the coffee table, Dad."

There was silence for a while and then I heard the TV go back on. He walked into the bedroom. "How's it going, girls?"

"OK, Dad."

"Fine, Mr. Frankle."

He stood watching us for a while and then went back to the living room. He was so restless. I could hear him moving around as I sorted through the papers. I tried to remember what it was like when Mother was here. They hadn't kept up nonstop conversations. Many times she would be sitting in the big chair reading a book, not even talking. Why wasn't my being in the house company enough to keep Dad contented?

He came into the room again. This time he had his coat on. "Since you girls are going to be busy all evening, I'm going out for a while. See you later."

He left. Joyce looked over at me. I got busy shuffling papers. I didn't want to talk about anything but the work we were doing.

He couldn't find a place for himself all weekend. He was in and out of the house a dozen times until we finally went out for our usual Chinese dinner on Sunday night.

Monday he called from the office. "Can you eat with your grandmother tonight?" He hesitated. "I'm going out to dinner

with some people." Again there was a pause. "They're bringing a friend for me."

I didn't know what I was supposed to say. I guessed it was a
female friend; I didn't think he'd bother to tell me if ten men
were going.

I must be a masochist. At dinner, Grandma asked me
where Daddy was. "He has a date," I answered.

She ripped a piece of bread in half. "See, I told you.
Men!" She said "men" the way someone else would say "ro-
dents." Though right now I was so turned off by Kenny that I
didn't blame her.

During the week Dad came home with a couple of new
suits. He mentioned seeing the Degas exhibit at the Metropoli-
tan Museum of Art. That really burned me up. Mother loved
art exhibits. She used to go with her ladies' groups because
Dad always said they were boring.

A couple of weeks flew by quickly. My suntan faded and
the only reminder was the thin white outline from my bikini.
December already. Grandma insisted that we go to services
with her the first night of Chanukah. Aunt Nina was coming
in from New York.

I was ready for a family holiday. Dad had been going out
quite a lot, ever since that restless weekend. I had been busy
too. Joyce and I had worked on the yearbook and she had per-
suaded me to go to a couple of parties. They weren't bad. I'd
dance with some fellows. It was almost fun until I'd catch a
glimpse of Kenny. Some women called the house and I was
always careful to get their names and phone numbers. No
more ripping up notes. Dad looked a lot happier. He didn't
drag up the steps and his jackets didn't hang. I was glad but I

kept wondering about Mother. He couldn't have forgotten her. Or was it like Grandma said?

I always liked Chanukah. While all my Christian friends were content with the loot from December twenty-fifth, I felt luckier because I collected gifts for eight days, each night we lit the Chanukah lights. Then there were potato latkes, delicious fried potato pancakes swimming in a plate of applesauce or sour cream. I don't know how pancakes got tied up with Chanukah. I couldn't imagine Judah Maccabee and his soldiers frying latkes while they fought the Romans. However they got together, Chanukah and potato latkes are inseparable.

I would say the blessings. Our menorah was an old one. Mom and Dad had brought it home from a trip to Israel. It was brass, like Grandma's candlesticks. There were two branches of carved metal that ended in eight flowerlike candle holders. Right in the middle was a taller branch. That was for the shamus, the candle that is lit first, then used to light the others, starting from the left, one for each night. On the last night the whole menorah would be lit and glowing.

After the blessings, we would sing. I would collect my gifts and then the latkes. I always had something for my parents and Grandma, made at the school arts-and-crafts program and always red or green, the Christmas colors of December. My father still has a green clay ashtray with the shape of my eight-year-old hand pressed on the bottom. And in our kitchen, Mother had hung macaroni-trimmed plates, pipestem hooks, and papier-mâché figurines that traced my school growth.

Dad came home with Aunt Nina. It was the first time I had seen her since we came back from Florida. There was no hesitation. She threw her arms around me and gave me a big hug. The gold bangle danced on her arm. I buried my head in her neck. She smelled absolutely delicious. No wonder no man could resist her. Grandma was directing traffic.

"Steven, you go upstairs and wash and come right down. Beth, is that what you're wearing tonight? Nina, come hurry, the latkes are going to get cold."

"Latkes, Mom?" Aunt Nina laughed. "I have to fit into a white maillot bathing suit for a cruise layout, and you're going to feed me latkes?"

"You they put in bathing suits! I'll never figure out why. If you don't fit they can use a medical school skeleton, the same thing!" Grandma gave Aunt Nina a playful shove.

Dad went into the bathroom to shave.

"Oh, by the way, Beth, I have regards for you."

I turned. "From whom, Dad?"

"Stacy Arnold. You remember Stacy?"

I wouldn't need an "I remember" in a yearbook to remember Stacy Arnold.

"She's been up on some business for Marty a couple of days this week and we had dinner."

I didn't know what I was supposed to say.

"I got some show tickets and we went dancing."

My father, the Don Juan. I still didn't say anything.

"She went back this morning. Comes up to New York every few months."

Terrific, I thought. Maybe we can have her for dinner. Grandma would adore her.

"Beth?" He caught my arm. "Anything wrong?"

I felt like a rat. He was reading my mind. "Beth, it's just going out." He shook the razor in the sink. "It doesn't mean anything. Just a night out, some laughs, conversation. I can't bury myself." He waved his arm around the room. "It's just too damn empty in this house."

I had a lump in my throat. I knew what he meant. It was empty for me too. And now if he was taking himself out of the house there would be nothing for me to hold on to. No matter how hard I had tried, I hadn't been able to fill up the house for him.

The phone rang. It was Mrs. Benson. "Hi, Beth, is your father home?" I had to answer yes, since he was standing right next to me and raising his eyebrows in a silent question as to who was on the phone.

He took it out of my hand. "Hi, Anita. No, I've been fine." Pause. He winked at me and loosened his tie. "Your note?" He looked puzzled. "I don't think I ever saw it. Beth and I were in Florida over Thanksgiving." Pause. "Oh, you know?" Pause. "Yeah, well maybe it got shuffled around someplace." Pause. "OK, swell, I'll look for you tonight."

"What was that all about?" I asked as he hung up the phone.

"Oh, nothing." His tie landed on the couch. "She says she sent me a note a few weeks ago, I guess about her single parents' club or wine-and-cheese parties—some nonsense like that."

He would never dream that I had ripped up his mail. I felt sorry for Mrs. Benson. "Dad, I guess her clubs are the only social life she has." Thinking about Stacy Arnold in action made me realize what a suburban lady like Mrs. Benson was up against. And the female voices that were calling this house sounded the way Stacy Arnold looked!

"Say, Beth, what are your plans for Christmas vacation?"

My plans? Since when did I have plans? "I don't know—hang around, I guess. Joyce'll be here. I have a term paper due in January that I should work on. Maybe I could go into the city and see a show or something."

"Great. Let me know about the show and I'll get you tickets. For Joyce too. What about Kenny?"

Dad hadn't been home enough to notice that Kenny was no longer calling. "Would you mind if I took a couple of days and went skiing? By myself. We'll go away again for Easter vacation, you and I. But I'd just like a little time away."

I told myself not to be upset. My father was a grown man and needed time to be by himself. But I was sick of people asking me if it was OK to do something and then doing it anyway.

"Oh, that's OK, Dad. Sure, go ahead! I'll keep busy during vacation."

We had dinner with Grandma and Aunt Nina and went to synagogue together. Except Aunt Nina. She told Grandma, "Rosh Hashanah, Yom Kippur, and the Israel Bond Dinner. They're the only times I go." Grandma sighed, but she had given up fighting Aunt Nina over synagogue a long time ago.

Joyce was there with her family, and we signaled each other during the sermon. After the services I joined her at a refreshment table in the back of the auditorium. The women of the sisterhood had made potato pancakes. They had been reheated and were greasy and heavy. At least they felt that way going down.

I saw Mrs. Benson approach Daddy. She had him backed against a corner of the stage and was talking earnestly, waving her arms.

Joyce saw them too. "I wasn't going to say anything, Beth, because I know how touchy you get, but Mrs. Benson has been asking my mother all kinds of questions about your dad."

I tossed my hair back. "You know what, Joyce? My father's a big boy; he can take care of himself."

Joyce smiled. "Well, what have we here? A changeover— you're not going to baby-sit for your father any more?"

Is that what she thought I had been doing? Baby-sitting for my father? I glanced over again. He caught my eye. I could tell by the way he inclined his head that he wanted to be rescued from Mrs. Benson. How did I know? It was a gesture I had seen him use many times with Mother. We would be at a family outing or something. He would tilt his head slightly to the side, the same as now, and send my mother a secret signal with his eyes. She would walk over and make up some excuse to get him out of the conversation. I guess the signal couldn't have been too secret if I had picked it up. Now I just waved at him, then turned my back, pretending I didn't notice his exasperation. If he was going to spend time at art exhibits and skiing, then he could spend five minutes being polite to Mrs. Benson. She was human, too—though for the life of me I couldn't figure out how Mrs. Benson and I got on the same side.

Sixteen

Two *days before Daddy left on his skiing vacation,* Grandma handed me a large piece of cardboard. "Here, it came with the mail. It wouldn't fit in the box, so the postman rang the bell."

It was one of those large postcards from Florida. Attached to the card was a net bag, filled with candy oranges. The message on the card read: "Steve—hope the cold inspires you more than the heat did! See you at the lodge. Stacy."

"Who is this Stacy? And what does this mean about hot and cold?"

"Grandma, you know you're not supposed to read other people's messages!"

"Who read it? It's right there for the whole world to see. I had to look to find out who the card was for, didn't I? Besides, you want something to be secret, you seal it in an envelope."

I knew from experience that sealing an envelope didn't

always keep a message secret. I was surprised at the card though.

Dad hadn't been keeping secrets from me. I knew when he went out. But he hadn't mentioned anything about Stacy Arnold being at the ski lodge with him. No wonder he didn't invite me along. A sixteen-year-old daughter cramps your style. Maybe Stacy wanted me to know. Otherwise, why didn't she write to his office?

Grandma tried again. "Who is this Stacy?"

"She works for a friend of Daddy's. He met her in Florida."

"Is she pretty?"

"Pretty? Huh! Is the Pope Catholic?"

"What do you mean? Who asked about the Pope?"

"Oh, Grandma, that's just an expression. Yes, Stacy's pretty. As a matter of fact, she's gorgeous."

"I knew it!"

I shouldn't have said anything. She was getting all wound up. "My poor Janet. Not a year yet, dead. And already dates, Florida, ski lodges. *Men,* you can't trust them."

"Gram, please, I have homework!"

"You know what, Beth?" I didn't know what, but I was sure I wouldn't like it.

"What, Gram?"

"When your father comes home from his skiing, I think I'll have that nice Mrs. Benson for dinner."

"But you said she was after Daddy."

"Never mind. At least I know she's in the neighborhood and she belongs to synagogue and the P.T.A. and has two nice kids. Just because she and her husband broke up, it's no reason to neglect her. Besides, Mrs. Benson I can handle. People that write notes about hot and cold and have names like Stacy, I can't do anything about."

Poor Mrs. Benson. I should warn her. If Grandma were going to take her side she wouldn't have a chance.

Dad was packing when I gave him the card from Stacy. He read it but never said a word. I vowed that I wasn't going to ask him if she was going.

He promised to bring me a souvenir. That did it. "I'm not your little girl anymore, Dad. I don't need a stuffed animal from a ski lodge."

He closed his suitcase. "Sit down, Beth."

"What for?" I was already sorry I had opened my mouth. I didn't want to hear what he was going to say.

"Yes, Stacy Arnold is meeting me in Vermont. There are four couples going, some fellows from my office. I should have told you."

"I don't care. It's none of my business." I was mumbling.

"Yes, it is your business. I guess I felt guilty about leaving you home alone."

"You don't have to feel guilty."

"Sure I do. Just like you feel guilty."

My head shot up.

"Hey, Beth." He put his arms around me. "Don't you think I realize that you've been giving up things to stay near me? I know something happened with Kenny too." He stood me up. "But Janet—your mother's—gone and we've both got to put it together from here. Stacy's fun. She's easy to be with. She makes me feel young. But the best thing of all is that she doesn't expect anything from me. No promises, no permanent ties, just some good times."

Four stars for Stacy Arnold!

He reached for his coat. "I want both you and me to try to have fun on this vacation, loosen up. And if your grandmother's on your back about me, tell her to save her money. She won't be making any weddings for me." He gave me a hug. "Feel better?"

I nodded.

"I'm not looking for anyone to replace your mother. But we both have to keep moving forward, Beth. Besides, you'll go off to college soon, and what'll you do with a father hanging over you to cramp your style?"

It's funny. I was worried about cramping his style and he had used the same words to me. Grandma had forgotten something. Dad might be able to get another woman, but he only had one daughter.

Christmas vacation started. I was going to sleep halftime at Joyce's and she was going to sleep halftime with me. Kenny was still hot and heavy with Rhoda.

Joyce tried to help. "Look, Beth, he's leaving anyway in February to go to college."

"How could he forget so quickly?"

"Who said he forgot? Maybe he just doesn't want to remember."

While I was busy trying to figure that out, she forced me into a blind date which was less than memorable. However, we were both in hysterics all night as I recited the mishaps that occurred. Sometime between two and three A.M., as we were having our third hot chocolate, I realized I was having fun.

It still hurt to think about Kenny, but I guess I didn't have to hurt all the time. I was entitled to have a little fun without signing a lifetime contract too.

On the third day of vacation I was having a light lunch with Grandma when Aunt Nina flew in. And that's a good description. She dropped packages on the couch and floor and tossed her fur coat over a chair. It missed.

Grandma jumped up. "Nina, I didn't expect you." They exchanged kisses. "Sit down and eat. I'll make you a tuna. No, grilled cheese. You like grilled cheese better."

"No thanks, Ma, I had a bite before I left the city."

"How come you're home, Aunt Nin? Not growing hair again, are you?"

She laughed. "No, thank goodness. I'm having a fight with my agent."

"What kind of fight?" we both asked together.

"Oh, another gal at the agency got a commercial that should have been mine. So I canceled my bookings for today."

"Nina," Grandma said, "why did you do that? What about the people who were depending on you today?"

"Too bad." Aunt Nina moved the thin gold bangle up and down her arm. "I left my apartment and didn't tell anyone where I was going. Let them all go crazy looking for me."

Her voice wasn't gentle now; it was strong and sure. I never realized before that Aunt Nina was such a tough lady. She always acted like a fragile butterfly at home—crying to Mother or having Grandma do everything for her. Acting completely helpless. And she really wasn't. She knew exactly what she was doing, even by running away from today's work.

She pointed to Grandma. "If the phone rings and it's for me, say you don't know where I am."

"Nina . . ."

Her regular voice was back. "If you do that, Ma, I'll let you make me a grilled cheese."

Grandma was already buttering the bread.

"I know it sounds like I'm being a spoiled baby, Beth. But I'm in a tough business. Sometimes you have to pull a tantrum or two to show them you mean what you say."

That was something to think about. Grandma was due for another blood pressure checkup next week. I wouldn't say anything now. But the next time Aunt Nina tried to persuade me to take over one of her responsibilities I was going to remember what a tiger she really was.

I wondered if Mother had ever known.

Seventeen

Dad called once from Vermont. I was out. Grandma gave me the message. "Your father says to tell you he's having a good time and wishes us all a happy New Year."

"Is he going to call back?"

Grandma sniffed. "How should I know? I just take messages around here."

Joyce and I were going to a party New Year's Eve. She had fixed me up with another blind date. It wasn't completely blind. The guy went to South Orange and I knew what he looked like. Still, a total stranger for New Year's Eve. It wasn't what I had planned.

"What's the difference?" asked Joyce. "New Year's Eve or Saturday night? Besides, there'll be a bunch of kids at the party so you can switch around if you don't hit it off."

Well, as long as he wasn't a basketball player!

December thirty-first was dark and dreary. It had snowed

during the week, but rain and the snowplows had turned white
to dirty slush. Aunt Nina was home. She went into a depression every New Year's Eve.

"I can't stand parties—everyone jumping around pretending to have a good time. Grandma and I will watch the ball
drop on TV and have a glass of Manischewitz at twelve
o'clock."

"New Year's Eve can't be that bad, Aunt Nina."

"It's never lived up to my expectations, so I've learned to
skip the whole thing."

I went back upstairs. I kept looking around our apartment
for something. I couldn't put my finger on it. Something that
belonged to December thirty-first. I realized what I was looking for when I passed the hall table. Every New Year's Eve
Daddy had sent Mother a dozen yellow roses. They would
stand on the table, tight buds at first, and then slowly open
over the week. The sweet smell stayed in the hall even after
they had started to wilt.

Mom would tease. "Steve, yellow roses in winter! They
must cost a fortune!"

Grandma would shake her head and say, "*Meshugah!* You
could have bought a scarf or blouse for what these cost." But
she too would bury her head in the sweet fragrance.

I remember Mother yelling at me when I was about ten.
The roses were in a crystal vase and I broke one off and put it
in a glass. I put the glass next to my bed. "Who took a rose?"
yelled Mother. I admitted it. She was very annoyed. She took
the rose out of the glass and stuck it back in the vase. I had
broken the stem in the middle and it wouldn't reach the water.

"Look," she said, "I share everything else in this house.

But these are my roses. Daddy sent them and they're very special."

I think I cried, because the next day I found a tiny pot of African violets with a note that said, "Happy New Year to Beth. Love, Daddy and Mommy." I overwatered the violets and they died. I didn't care because I knew they weren't as special as the yellow roses.

And now no yellow roses because there was no more Mother. And no matter what he said, I wasn't even sure I had a father anymore with all the running around he seemed to be doing.

The house was stripped of everything that had belonged to Mother. And despite his speech about us moving on together, if Daddy forgot that *she* existed, what about *me?*

Suddenly I had to get close to her. Looking at pictures didn't do it. A black-and-white image caught on a piece of paper wasn't Mother.

I ran back down to Aunt Nina. Luckily, Grandma wasn't around. "Hey, Aunt Nina, would you do me a special favor?"

"If I can."

"Would you drive me to the cemetery?"

I could see her hesitate. None of us had been to the cemetery since the funeral. It was another Jewish custom. You weren't supposed to go back before a year had passed. That's when you had an unveiling of the tombstone. Grandma was already talking about different-sized stones.

For once Aunt Nina didn't try to get out of it. "I'll get my coat," she said. "But you better put boots on, Beth. It'll be freezing out there."

We drove in silence. It was about a twenty-five-minute

ride down the Garden State Parkway. Aunt Nina jingled the
thin gold bangle. "Beth, I hope you don't mind, but I'll sit
in the car and wait for you. I just couldn't take seeing her
grave . . ."

"That's OK, Aunt Nin." I didn't want to tell her I was
glad. I wanted to be alone and had been wondering how to ask
for privacy.

It was very cold. The snow was piled up in drifts over the
graves. But at least it was white snow, clean snow that the city
pollution hadn't gotten to. Aunt Nina parked the car and
pointed to the row that Mother was lying in. No one had been
in this part of the cemetery since the snowstorm. I made the
first footprints. I walked slowly, trying to find the path under
the snow and afraid to step directly on the graves.

I read the inscriptions on headstones as I walked. I didn't
remember seeing any of them the day of the funeral.

"Earl Carver, beloved son, age 2 months. D. 1974." Sad,
to lose a two-month-old baby. But then again his parents
didn't have that long to love him.

"Rest in Peace. Stanley and Molly Silver. Beloved parents,
grandparents, and sister and brother."

My mother was a daughter, a mother, a wife, and a sister.
She didn't live long enough to be a grandmother. But then
little Earl Carver had only lived long enough to be a son.

There was my grandfather's grave. "Louis Bernstein, beloved husband, father, and grandfather, died May 5, 1970."
The empty space next to him was saved for my grandmother.
Next to that was a small wooden marker. "Janet Frankle, Sept.
1977." You didn't get the beloveds until you got the permanent stone.

If there is anyplace to go after leaving this life, at least Mother was there with her father. My feet were freezing. I stamped the ground. But then I had been freezing and trembling at the funeral, and the warm sun had been shining. I noticed something sticking out of the snow at the top of the grave. It looked like a ribbon. I bent over and brushed the snow away. It was a bouquet. One dozen long-stemmed roses. They must have been left last week, before the snowstorm. The petals had frozen and they flaked off as I moved the stems. But you could still tell the color. They were yellow. I broke one off and put it in my pocket. I laid the rest back on the grave. I didn't think Mother would mind if I kept one this time.

I walked back to the car with my fingers wrapped around the crumbling flower. So extravagant. Yellow roses in the middle of winter. I hoped Dad would call again. He needed the change. If the skiing was good, I would tell him to take some extra time in Vermont.